MURDER IN METROPOLIS

MURDER IN METROPOLIS

To Laura,
Welcome to Metropolis !
Lonnie

LONNIE CRUSE

Quiet Storm Publishing • Martinsburg, WV

Published by Quiet Storm Publishing
PO BOX 1666
Martinsburg, WV 25402

www.quietstormpublishing.com

Cover by Clint Gaige

ISBN: 0-9749608-96

LCCN: 2003090742

This is a work of fiction. Any resemblance to actual
events or persons, living or dead, is entirely coincidental.

Printed in the United States of America

DEDICATION

For NATHAN—whose frequent enthusiastic visits to the Superman statue sparked the idea for this story.

And DANIEL—little brother following so closely in big brother's footsteps.

With all my love.

ACKNOWLEDGEMENTS

A special "Thank You!" to Massac County Sheriff Bob Griffey and his staff, Coroner Steve Farmer, Paducah Police Department Detective Rob Estes, Doctor Shawn Jones, Doctor Mitzi Richardson DVM, Authors C. D. Blizzard, G. Miki Hayden, and Bonnie Hearn Hill, Support Team Don Cruse, Debby Biles, Ann Brewer, Pam Windhorst, Patrick Windhorst, and above all, Clint Gaige and the staff at Quiet Storm Publishing. Couldn't have done it without 'cha!

Lonnie Cruse 2003

DISCLAIMER

While the city of Metropolis, Illinois does exist, perched as it were on the edge of the Ohio River, eyeball to eyeball with Paducah, Kentucky, the characters in this story are entirely fictional and are not intended to represent anyone living or dead. And while I have described Metropolis as accurately as possible, be advised I DID take some poetic license and "moved" a building or two downtown. No facades were damaged during this move.

CHAPTER 1

Sheriff Joe Dalton plunked his boots on top of his desk, leaned back in the protesting chair, snapped open his newspaper, and hooked a finger through his donut-shaped coffee cup. Before he could down a swig, the intercom buzzed, forcing him to wade under a stack of files and punch a button.

"Yes, George?"

"We've got a situation outside on Market Street, Sheriff. Guess you'll have to handle it," the elderly dispatcher informed him. "Morning shift hasn't arrived yet, and the night deputies are still at that big accident scene over on Highway 145."

"Would the situation outside be Big Ed Simmons?"

"Yes, sir; drunk as they come and singing fair to wake the dead."

"Where is he this time? The courthouse steps?"

"Nope. The steps at Lipinski's Appliances again. Miz Lipinski says if we don't shut him up, she will, with that old pistol her husband kept in the store. Though what an eighty-year-old woman with crippling arthritis is doing with—"

"I'll get right on it, George. We don't need Mrs. Lipinski shooting up Market Street at day break."

Dalton dropped the newspaper on his desk, hiked his pants toward his spare tire, and reached for his cup. No sense in letting the coffee get cold. Big Ed would come along peacefully. He always did. Like as not, he was purposely upsetting

10

Mrs. Lipinski so she'd report him again, netting him a bed in a warm cell or a free ride home.

Dalton elbowed his way through the heavy glass door of the Massac County Detention Center into the early morning darkness, keeping his coffee cup steady with his left hand and pulling his jacket collar up with his right. Wouldn't be long before winter weather took over.

He cringed as the massive door banged shut behind him, the sound echoing loudly across the empty, windswept street. Time to turn in another request to Kevin. Dalton toyed briefly with the idea of handcuffing the unresponsive maintenance man to the front door in the futile hope that it might somehow speed up the repairs.

A gust of chill wind raked the few remaining leaves off the nearby trees, swooshing them up in the air in a macabre, ghost-like dance. Dalton's gaze followed the flight of the leaves to the nearby rooftops. He wondered if the thick clouds he saw above would drop a much-needed rain on the area before they passed by. The streetlights, Victorian era replicas, cast a soft glow in the early morning darkness.

Dalton's gaze dropped to his right, toward the courthouse, which still slept in the semi-darkness. The old building, situated catty-corner to his office, looked like a sister to the many other small town courthouses scattered across the Midwest. Built in the early forties, it was surrounded by aged, red brick; fussy concrete trim; and concrete steps that marched up to each entrance. Large trees, now robbed of their glory by the stealthy autumn wind, stood sentry nearby.

Dalton could hear the off-key solo long before he crossed Market Street and reached the steps where Big Ed Simmons, once the town's most successful lawyer but now its most successful drunk, huddled in the stairwell.

Mrs. Lipinski had lived in the apartment over the appliance store for as long as Dalton could remember. Whenever

Big Ed couldn't find his way home, he would seek shelter in her stairwell; he was not a welcome guest.

"Come on, Big Ed, I'll take you to my office for some coffee. It's too cold for you to be out here. The night shift will be over soon. One of my deputies can take you home." Dalton swallowed a sip of his own coffee.

"What's he doing up there, Sheriff?" Big Ed bellowed in a voice that made him sound much larger than he actually was. "Showing off, or is he drunker than me? You probably should arrest him too."

"Nobody gets drunker than you, Big Ed. What do I think who is doing?"

Big Ed smiled crookedly at the left-handed compliment. His tailor-made suit was wrinkled and dirty, and Dalton wondered if he'd lost his ties along with everything else when his fed-up wife had taken him to the cleaners.

"Him." Big Ed gestured loosely toward the enormous Superman statue that nearly dwarfed the east end of the old courthouse. The town fathers had placed it there after the Illinois state legislature had officially tagged Metropolis as Superman's home.

"Jack Hatfield, the guy that likes to pretend he's Superman. What's he doing on the statue?" The smell of sour beer wafted its way up to Dalton's nose.

Dalton turned to look in the direction Big Ed pointed and saw that Jack Hatfield—dressed in his Superman costume—dangled over the statue's huge right wrist, half his body on one side, half on the other. At least the figure looked like Jack. From where he stood, Dalton couldn't see exactly who was draped there since the red cape hung in the way.

An alarm bell went off in Dalton's head, and the chill that ran up his back had nothing to do with the frost-tinged breeze.

"Don't know, but I aim to find out."

As far as Dalton knew, Jack Hatfield had never been drunk

a day in his life. If it was his old friend, something must be terribly wrong for him to be hanging there like that. And how on earth had he gotten up there? The statue was as slick as a greased telephone pole, and the arm was at least ten feet off the ground. No way anyone could climb it without help.

A few steps across the street, Dalton saw blood dripping off the body, down the large blue leg of the statue, and onto the concrete foundation below. The blood had oozed into the words "Truth, Justice, and the American Way", turning the lettering a dull red-brown.

Dalton broke into a run. He heard the sound of his favorite cup smashing on the pavement. His mind focused on the hot liquid burning its way through his pant leg because he didn't want to accept what his eyes were seeing.

Heart pounding, Dalton raced up the ramp to the statue and came to a skidding halt. He stood frozen to the spot for a full minute.

Jack Hatfield's head, its dark hair matted with blood, had been neatly severed from his body and placed on the large concrete letter S beneath Superman, staring sightlessly at the statue of the character he'd imitated for so many years.

As Dalton reached for his radio to call for backup, he felt like a weight the size of a loaded river barge had just dropped onto his chest.

"George, are any of the deputies in the office yet?"

"Yes, sir; morning shift just came in."

"Send them outside to the statue. There's a problem out here, and I want this area secured now."

"Yes, sir." The dispatcher's high-pitched voice went up an octave. "What is it? What's happened?"

"Fill you in later."

Dalton was in no mood to chat. Besides, Means knew better than to ask for details. At least half the county would be listening in on the law enforcement band over morning coffee,

13

eager for any interesting tidbits about what had happened during the night. Well, they wouldn't get them from him just yet, at least not by eavesdropping in on his radio.

His cell phone was still recharging somewhere on his desk, so Dalton walked a few feet away from the statue to the pay phone, dropped in some coins, woke up the coroner, and told him to alert the crime lab technicians in Carbondale. Using the pay phone instead of his radio should keep curious civilians from swarming the courthouse square before the crime lab technicians arrived.

Despite the heavy cloud cover, it was getting lighter. Courthouse employees would be coming to work soon, as would the shop owners and store clerks on Market Street. Dalton knew he and his deputies would have to work fast to get the entire courthouse square taped off and the investigation started before curious onlookers surrounded them. Metropolis, Illinois had never seen anything like this.

Someone was bound to alert the local media, and they would be on the scene minutes later, possibly before the crime lab technicians who had much farther to drive. A story like this would probably bring out the national media as well.

Dalton walked slowly back to the base of the statue to wait for his deputies. He forced himself to clamp a lid on the sick anger threatening to boil over and pondered how he could possibly have missed spotting the dead body draped there. True, he usually ignored the impressive replica of Superman, as did most of the locals—it was only the tourists who stopped to gawk and cause traffic jams—but this was something he shouldn't have missed.

Dalton looked up at the fifteen-foot tall bronze figure of the comic book hero: red-booted legs spread wide, hands on hips, red cape seeming to billow in the breeze, and dark eyes keeping watch on Market Street. He wondered what those eyes had seen last night.

14

Sheriff Joe Dalton had just gotten the most important case of his entire career. The thought gave him no satisfaction.

CHAPTER 2

Dalton turned at the sound of the detention center door slamming and watched his deputies walk toward the statue, carrying equipment. Dispatcher George Means followed closely behind them, obviously trying to grab a quick look-see at the crime scene, his long nose pointed in the air like an old coon dog fresh on the scent. Dalton moved briskly back across the street to where Big Ed Simmons still shivered in the stairwell and motioned for Means to follow him.

"George, escort Big Ed back to my office and give him plenty of hot coffee to drink. And don't leave your post again."

"Yes, sir." Means audibly sniffed at the sight and smell of Big Ed, but did as he was ordered. Dalton had taken steps early on to make certain his staff understood that any overt signs of mutiny would earn the offender a swift keelhauling from the sheriff.

Dalton left Means grappling with Big Ed and walked back to the huddle of deputies staring open-mouthed at the form still hanging on the statue. Deputy Doody Jenson's flaming face matched his hair. He was obviously fighting to keep from being sick and losing the battle. Dalton took pity on him.

"Doody, make a sweep of the courthouse square. Don't disturb anything, just take a good look around."

"Yes, sir." Waddling toward the north end of the court-house, Doody looked like a grown up, overweight version of the famous fifties puppet. George Means daily joke of greeting the deputy with "Howdy, Doody" had long since worn thin with Dalton, but the nickname had stuck.

"I'd better go around the opposite side, in case Doody misses something," Billy Wilson offered. "He looks like he's about to lose it."

Dalton nodded and Wilson moseyed off with the loose-limbed gait of a former star basketball player.

"And see if you can find the janitor's ladder. The killer could have used it to get the body up there. I don't see him bringing one along."

"Will do," Wilson responded over his shoulder.

Dalton turned to the other deputies and found Craig Edwards's thin shoulders hunched over, fingers struggling to tie his end of the yellow tape to the black railing around the statue. Linda Peters yanked the roll out of Edwards's hand, tied the knot, and passed the tape back to him, shaking her blond ponytail back and forth.

"You'd think that with a houseful of boys, Craig would be used to the sight of blood. Somebody's nearly always falling or fighting in his bunch." The sturdy mother of two snorted at her fellow deputy and began to tie her own end of the tape to the rail.

"Let Edwards rope off the square," Dalton said. "I need you to take measurements and pictures of the scene. I'll help. I want to get that job done so the coroner can take the body down as soon as possible."

Peters nodded and reached for the camera case. She stepped carefully around the pool of blood at Superman's feet. Dalton walked slowly around his half of the large statue, holding one end of the metal measuring tape, and looking for evidence as he walked. It was the job of the crime lab team to collect, bag, and label all the evidence, but he wanted to be certain nothing important was overlooked in this investigation.

Dalton's sympathies were with the two male officers who were fighting nausea. He wondered why raising kids seemed to give women a stronger stomach than men. They certainly appeared to be better able to deal with body fluids, in their various, unappetizing forms, than most men were.

Don Jeffords's van swept up to the courthouse, and the young coroner hopped out to unload the stretcher. The Jeffords family owned the oldest funeral home in Metropolis and had been burying residents for several decades. Dalton was willing to bet dollars to donuts that none of the Jeffords clan had ever seen a corpse like this one.

Dalton watched Jeffords gape at the figure on the arm of the statue and then swallow hard.

"Who could have done this?" Jeffords began then lapsed into shocked silence.

"I don't have any idea, but I'm going to find out if it takes me the rest of my life," Dalton responded. "As soon as the crime lab team gives the okay, get him down from there and cover him up."

Jeffords nodded, still gazing openmouthed at the statue.

The color of the sky had shifted slowly from dull black to dirty gray. Out of the corner of one eye, Dalton watched the crowd around the courthouse grow larger. Local businessmen and county employees stood shoulder to shoulder with early customers and courthouse visitors, staring at the statue in fascinated horror. Photographers from the Metropolis Planet, Paducah Sun, and the Vienna Times jostled each other in an effort to get that front-page photo. The NewsChannel 6 team busily cranked up the rooftop antennae on their van to send a direct feed for the morning newscast.

Movement at Dalton's elbow drew his attention away from the crowd to where Deputy Edwards was tucking in the last of the bright yellow tape.

"Make sure everyone stays outside the tape until the crime lab team arrives and that includes the courthouse employees. When the head tech is satisfied that the front steps are clean, we'll log people in and out through that door. Keep the east entrance secured until the techs pack up and leave."

Edwards nodded and turned to the task.

"Where's Jenson and Wilson?" Dalton's eyes swept over the area. He spotted Doody Jenson in front of the large, near-naked bushes at the north end of the courthouse, his head low, and his large posterior pointed toward the sky.

"Found something, Sheriff." Wilson rounded the south end of the building. "The janitor's ladder is in the stairwell, back where he always keeps it. There's blood on several of the rungs."

Great. At least his staff had found some solid evidence. Dalton swiped his hand across his forehead.

The crime lab technicians spilled out of their van and began to cover the courthouse square like eager ants in search of their winter food supply. Unfortunately, the first thing they spotted was Deputy Jenson being sick in the bushes. Jonesy, the head crime lab technician, made quite a show of wanting to collect the "evidence." Any other day Dalton would have enjoyed Jonesy's graveyard humor. Not today.

"Wilson found the janitor's ladder with bloodstains on it. Hopefully that'll give you guys some clue as to the killer's identity," Dalton said through clenched teeth.

Jonesy shrugged and followed Wilson to the back of the courthouse.

Jeffords joined Dalton at the base of the statue. The young coroner's short, compact build was generally up to handling bodies of any size, but this corpse was proving to be more of a challenge than he could handle alone. The cool weather had caused rigor mortis to come on slowly and was letting it leave just as slowly; and the opening in the statue's arm where the body had been shoved wasn't all that large.

Dalton radioed Means to contact the fire department for the nearest ladder truck. With the firefighters' help, Jeffords managed to get Hatfield's body down off Superman's arm, onto the sidewalk, and place it on a clean white evidence sheet.

"Quite a sight, isn't it?" Dalton asked. He knelt down beside the coroner as if to help him place the body in the black bag. In reality he wasn't going to touch the corpse.

"I want to know who did this." Dalton dropped his voice, not wanting any of the nearby gawkers to overhear. "We're obviously dealing with a very sick mind here. I've never seen anything this vicious. We've both lived here our entire lives; who do we know who is capable of cutting off a man's head and putting his body on public display like this?"

Jeffords shook his head at the rhetorical question.

"Anything you or the forensic pathologist can come up with will be a big help. We have to find this guy fast, before he has a chance to strike again."

Jeffords nodded. "Couldn't agree with you more. I can tell you one thing now. The decapitation isn't what killed him. Not enough blood on or around the body. He was strangled first, probably from behind. There's a clear mark just below one ear. With any luck, the pathologist will be able to tell you what he was strangled with."

"Strangled, huh?" Dalton forced himself to zip open the bag and take a close look at the head, something he hadn't been able to do before.

"Yep," Dalton agreed. "Face is swollen, tongue's sticking out. Missed that, pretty much kept my eyes on the back of his head."

"There are other body signs as well, so my guess is the pathologist will put that down as the cause of death."

The sight of his friend's bloody head made Dalton's scalp itch, and he ran a hand through his own thick crop. "I've been wondering how the killer managed to overpower Jack. He wasn't big, but he was strong. No way anybody could've taken him down head on. It had to be from behind."

"I'll stop by your office when I get back from Evansville and let you know what I've found out." Jeffords thumped Dalton's shoulder in the traditional male ritual of support and began placing the body on the stretcher.

Dalton watched as Jeffords loaded the dead man into the back of his van and headed down Market Street toward Highway 45. The nearest forensic pathologist was at the Vanderburgh County Coroner's office in Evansville, Indiana, a little less than two hours away.

In any case of suspected foul play, Jeffords's practice was to deliver the body there for the autopsy and stay with it while the procedure was performed. Dalton figured with any luck the coroner would be back in Metropolis by late afternoon with a preliminary report, ready and able to field questions from the media.

The forensic pathologist's facilities in Evansville were well equipped. If there was any evidence on the body that would help solve this murder, the pathologist would find it. Dalton could just imagine the f.p.'s face when he got a look at Jack Hatfield's remains.

When Jeffords returned, he would be ready to release the body to Hatfield's family so they could make the funeral arrangements. Dalton sighed. Jack's family. All that was left now was a younger brother and sister. Their parents had died in a murder/suicide scandal that had rocked the whole town years ago.

Well, someone had to tell them about Jack's murder. Ordinarily Dalton would send a deputy to break the bad news, but not this time. Jack Hatfield had been an old friend. Better the news should come firsthand from the sheriff.

Dalton ducked around the long fire truck, deftly avoiding

the media swarm, and strode up Market Street toward Seventh Street where Hatfield's Hardware stood. The second story of the old building housed an apartment, which Hatfield had shared with his brother Mark and sister Peggy. The first fat drops of rain pelted Dalton's uncovered head. The gloom of the sky matched his mood perfectly.

A few other stores on Market Street had apartments over them as well. Dalton had assigned Peters and Edwards to check with each of the occupants for possible witnesses to anything unusual the night before. Peters was good at drawing people out, and Edwards could spot a lie a mile away. Wilson was breaking the bad news to Ruby Miller, Hatfield's long-time girlfriend.

Doody, useless at the crime scene, had been sent back to the office to assist in sobering up and calming down Big Ed before he gave his statement as to what he'd seen that morning. The former legal eagle was the department's best hope of a witness, at least for the moment, and Dalton prayed that he wasn't too drunk to remember anything of value. Big Ed's memory tended to be about as reliable as the weather.

Dalton glanced in the store windows as he passed by. Some merchants were beginning to display Halloween decorations, even though the holiday was weeks away. Many of the downtown stores stayed open late on Halloween, and the kids went door-to-door to get treats from them or to soap the windows of the stores that had closed.

Jack had always dressed up in his Superman costume for the holiday, and he'd always had the best treats: popcorn balls, M & M's, Pez candy dispensers, and lots of loose change. Hatfield's Hardware was a favorite stop with kids for miles around. Dalton's own two children had always clamored to be taken there when they were young. Jack certainly wouldn't be treating anyone this year.

Dalton rounded the corner, carefully dodging a mound of

pigeon droppings and clanged up the metal stairway that led to the Hatfields' apartment.

CHAPTER 3

Peggy Hatfield came out of the bathroom dressed in an old, blue flannel robe tied loosely around her ample middle and floppy house shoes that slapped against her bare feet. She ran a hand through her short, sandy hair in an attempt to make it more presentable, but the effort only made it worse. Her face was flushed, apparently from the steamy water.

The pretty young girl Dalton had once known was lost somewhere in this worn-out, overblown woman. How long had it been since he'd seen her? A couple of years? Five, maybe?

Mark closed the hall door behind her, grabbed a suspender with his fist, and waited. The paper cup in his left hand held a dark, coffee-like liquid, most likely tobacco juice. Dalton had given up chewing tobacco when his wife threatened to move him into the garage. Apparently Mark wasn't quite as hen-pecked.

"I need to talk to both of you about Jack."

Dalton indicated the couch, and brother and sister trudged over to it. They sat down so heavily that Dalton wondered if the couch legs would survive. He squelched the sudden memory of two teenage boys sprawled on that very couch years ago, munching popcorn, and watching old westerns. Mark reached over and turned on a lamp.

Peggy mopped the sweat from her brow with the sleeve of her robe. "Mark says Jack didn't come home last night, and your being here this early means something's wrong. What is it?" She sounded short of breath.

Dalton sat down. "I'm very sorry to have to tell you both this, but there's no easy way. Jack was murdered sometime last night. We found his body this morning near the statue on the square."

Peggy crumpled into the folds of the couch. "I don't understand. It isn't possible."

Mark reached out, set his cup down, and put his hand over hers. His jaws moved slowly side to side.

"The investigation is just beginning, so we don't have a lot of information yet." Dalton answered. "I know it's a tough time, but I need to ask you both some questions."

"Okay." Peggy's hand shook as she wiped her eyes with a tissue fished from the depths of a huge pocket on the side of her bathrobe. "What do you want to know?"

"What time did Jack leave home last night?" Dalton asked.

"I don't know," Peggy said. "I had a migraine and went to bed early."

She glanced at Mark who spit into his cup and placed it back on the table. He spoke for the first time since she'd entered the room. "Jack went out a little after seven. Said he was meetin' some salesman to order stuff for the store."

"Why was he meeting a salesman after hours? Don't they usually come to the store during the day?"

Mark shrugged. "Yeah, but Jack said this guy was buying him dinner if he'd meet him after the store closed. Said the salesman couldn't make his rounds at the usual time. Dunno why,"

"How do you know it was after seven?" Dalton asked.

"I was watching TV when he left. My favorite show was on, Law and Order. Never miss it."

Dalton glanced at the television in the corner where the local weatherman mouthed silently from the muted screen and gestured at the clouds heading like a freight train straight toward Illinois, Kentucky, and Indiana, hauling a load of rain.

Might as well get the toughest questions out of the way. "Did either of you leave home at any time last night?"

"My head hurt too much to even sit in here, much less go out." Peggy's voice quavered. "And Mark was in the living room all evening. He would have let me know if he was going out."

"Can anyone else verify that you were both home?"

Brother and sister looked at each other and shook their heads.

"Don't get much company. You're the first one that's been up here in a long time," Mark answered.

Dalton turned to Mark. "And you're sure Jack didn't come home at all last night?"

"Pretty sure. I watched the late news and then went to bed. Jack wasn't home then. He sleeps—slept—in the bedroom at the far end of the hall. There's 'nother door to it off the kitchen. Mine's off the living room, so I don't usually hear him come in after I've gone to bed."

Mark let go of Peggy's hand and covered a cough. "When I didn't hear him getting ready for work this morning, I went to look. His bed ain't been touched. Figured he'd spent the night at Ruby's, least ways till I saw you at the back door."

"I know Jack and Ruby were close. Did he spend the night with her often?"

"He used to. Hasn't been staying as much lately. Thought they was about to break up." Mark scratched his stubbly cheek and then hunched over, elbows on knees, hands clasped loosely in front of him, and waited for Dalton's next question.

Peggy worried the tissue as she rocked gently side to side. She looked dazed. So did her younger brother. That wasn't a surprise. In spite of all his years of experience, Dalton still felt dazed himself.

"Any idea which salesman Jack might've had this meeting with?" The gas logs in the old fireplace were making the room warmer by the minute. Dalton was starting to sweat now that his damp uniform had dried out.

"Nope. Never said which one, just said he was meetin' someone. Said not to wait up," Mark answered.

"I need a list of all the salesmen who sold to Jack and their phone numbers. Can you get me one?"

"Yeah, sure. Jack kept a list in the cash register drawer." Mark cleared his throat. "Want me to run downstairs and get it now?"

"Not just yet. I'll go down there with you and have a look around in a few minutes. We can get it then."

Mark nodded agreement.

"You still haven't told us what happened to him, Joe," Peggy said. She pulled the lapels of her robe together and shivered in the overly warm room.

Dalton placed his pen and notebook back inside his jacket.

"I'll warn you that it's pretty gruesome, but word is bound to get out, and I'd rather you heard it from me."

There was no other way to say it but straight out. He took a deep breath and plunged in.

"The killer cut off Jack's head and placed it at the foot of the statue. His body was left hanging over Superman's arm."

Well, that was certainly tactful. No wonder his deputies always wanted to draw straws when it came to breaking the bad news to survivors.

Peggy grew so pale that Dalton was afraid she'd faint. To his relief, she sat up straighter. Mark studied the floor.

"There will have to be an autopsy, of course. Don Jeffords picked up the body and took it to Evansville. We'll get the preliminary results later this afternoon."

The clock on the mantle ticked away the seconds while Dalton gave them time to absorb the news. He looked at the pictures surrounding the clock for lack of anything better to do and wished himself to be just about anywhere else.

"Either one of you know any reason why someone would've wanted to kill Jack? Or leave him like that?" Dalton asked. "Did he have any enemies that you were aware of?"

"No," Mark said. "Far as I know, everyone in this town liked Jack, looked up to him even. He was the town hero."

Dalton glanced at Peggy.

"He never mentioned having any enemies to me. Like Mark said, everyone liked Jack." Her voice broke as the tears slid down her plump cheeks. "He hadn't been seeing as much of Ruby lately. I suppose they could have been having problems."

Something to look into, at least. But Ruby couldn't have placed Jack's body on the statue all by herself.

"Was there anything wrong with the store that you were aware of?" Dalton asked.

Mark shook his head. Peggy blew her nose into the tissue before answering.

"Jack had been acting different lately. There could've been problems with the store, but he never said if there were. He didn't like us asking a lot of questions."

"Do you know what shape the business is in financially? Did he leave a will or make any arrangements for you two if something happened to him? Did he have a lawyer?" Dalton hoped for some positive answers.

Peggy shook her head. "He never discussed the store with us. Said we wouldn't understand how the business was run. Said he'd take care of everything. I don't even know where to begin to find out." She swallowed a sob.

Uneasy in the face of her distress, Dalton turned back to Mark. "Did he take his Superman outfit with him when he left last night?"

"Don't see why he would," Mark answered. "He was wearing jeans and a long sleeve shirt, stuff he usually wore to work. Probably took his leather jacket. Only wore that stupid Superman suit at special times like Halloween or the Superman festival, times like that. Never wore it when he was workin'. Why do you ask?"

"He was wearing his costume when we found him this morning. I'd like to take a look at Jack's room and the clothes he wore last night, if they're here."

"Sure. I'll show you." Mark spit out the last of the tobacco and pushed himself off of the couch.

Dalton stood and patted Peggy's shoulder. "Why don't you get some rest? Don Jeffords will contact you later today about making the funeral arrangements. I'll be happy to help out any way I can."

"Thanks, Joe. I'll try."

Dalton turned to Mark. "I want you both to know that I will do everything I can to find out who did this to Jack."

Mark nodded and led the way through the hall door past his bedroom. The chair next to the old-fashioned dresser held carefully folded nightclothes. Mark sure kept his room neater than he kept himself. Unless Peggy took care of his room along with the rest of the house.

They passed another bedroom. The twin beds were more feminine than the beds in Mark's room, and the frilly ruffle around the edge of the vanity identified this room as Peggy's. The bedclothes were all askew.

Dalton realized he hadn't paid much attention to Mark or Peggy or their rooms when he'd hung out in this apartment so many years ago. He and Jack had been too busy being football heroes to bother with little brothers or sisters.

Between Peggy's room and her older brother's, the bathroom door stood open. Dalton remembered the claw-footed bathtub that still filled most of the small area. A pile of wet towels lay on the floor near the sink.

Jack had obviously taken over his parents' bedroom some

time after their deaths, leaving Mark the room at the other end of the hall. Mark was right. The bed didn't look as if it had been slept in the night before. Nice furniture. It certainly didn't look like a room where three people had died in a moment of jealous rage over two decades ago.

What had Harold Hatfield hoped to accomplish by shooting his wife and her lover, and then turning the gun on himself? Who had he thought would take care of his kids? Had he cared at all that his children's lives would be disrupted forever? Had he given any thought to who would find the bodies? No one had even known anything had happened until Jack had come home from school and found the three of them. It was the grisliest event in the town's history; or had been until this morning.

Mark turned on the closet light then stepped back for Dalton to look inside. The closet smelled of cedar and aftershave. Jack's clothes were all neatly hung. Everything in the closet was in apple pie order, just as Dalton had expected. Mark looked carefully for the clothes his brother had worn the night before, but they were nowhere to be found. The black leather jacket wasn't there nor, of course, the Superman costume.

"Is this where Jack always kept his Superman costume when he wasn't wearing it?" Dalton asked.

"Yep, right here in his closet on a special hanger that don't leave no marks." Mark pointed to the hanger.

"And you didn't see him take it with him when he left?"

"Nope. After he told me not to wait up, he went back to his room and out the kitchen door. Didn't notice if he had anything with him. I guess he could have grabbed it then, 'though I don't know why he'da taken it." Mark took off his ever-present ball cap with the Hatfield Hardware logo barely visible above the sweat ring, scratched his head, and put the hat back on.

"Well, Jack must've taken the costume with him and changed into it somewhere else. If we can locate his missing clothes, we might know where he spent part of his evening and possibly who killed him," Dalton said. "Does anything else appear to be missing or out of place?"

"Nope, not as far as I can tell," Mark replied.

Dalton took one final look around the bedroom, but didn't see the answers to the questions that were plaguing him. Why Jack? Why now? Why in so grisly a manner? And what was the connection with the Superman statue?

CHAPTER 4

Dalton listened as Mark Hatfield's key scraped in the old lock. Hatfield's Hardware, which should have been open for business nearly an hour ago, smelled dank, as if it had been closed for months instead of hours.

Mark flipped on the lights. Dalton half expected to see his old friend behind the counter at the cash register where he'd spent so much of his time. He could almost hear Jack's deep, rumbling laugh.

Mark walked stiffly over to the cash register and retrieved the list of salesmen that the store dealt with. He shut the drawer with a bang and jumped when something skittered out of sight behind a counter.

"Mice?" Dalton asked.

"Could be. We get 'em sometimes. I'll check the traps. Don't want nothing stinking up the place."

Mark handed the list to Dalton, grabbed a flashlight, and stooped down to look under the nearby counters. Apparently the traps were empty. Mark stood up again.

"Was there any money in the cash register?"

"Some, not much. Jack always left enough change in there to start business the next day. The rest he had me take to the bank every evening."

"Is there enough to take care of you and Peggy for a while?"

"Don't know. You'll have to ask her about that. I don't have much of a head for figures."

Dalton tapped the list against his thumb. "We'll contact each of these salesmen and see who was with Jack last night. Maybe he can shed some light on things." Dalton jammed the list into his jacket pocket.

"Maybe."

"I'd also like to look at the inventory list. See if anything is missing. It could be important." Dalton said.

"It's in the file cabinet in back, by the bathroom. I'll get it."

With Mark headed to the back of the store, Dalton had time to look around. Snow shovels and sleds were carefully hung on the wall behind the cash register. Bags of rock salt were stacked on the floor at one end of the counter, even though the first snow-flakes probably wouldn't fly until late December. Jack always liked to be ready way ahead of schedule.

Everything down there, as upstairs, was neat and orderly. Nothing out of place. No sign of a struggle. Jack must have left at closing time yesterday and never come back. The store sure seemed empty without him. The old building creaked under the force of the wind outside.

Mark returned with the inventory sheet and handed it to Dalton.

"Everything in the store is listed there. Jack kept careful records."

"There's no use counting every single nut and bolt in here. I really just want to check on the saws. I need to know if any are missing."

"They're on the shelves right against that wall or hanging on nails above. Put them there, myself. I'll help you count."

Dalton and Mark checked the inventory sheet carefully. Hatfields' Hardware sold every kind of saw imaginable—from crosscut and bow to electric jig. Enough variety to fill any carpenter's dreams. According to the figures on the inventory sheet, the saws were all present and accounted for.

"Look around carefully, Mark. Is there anything else missing?"

"If there is, I'll know it."

Mark and Dalton walked slowly up and down each aisle and around the bins. Mark shook his head.

"Everything's just like Jack always kept it. There's a lot of stuff in here, but if anything big was missing, I'd know. Been in here every day of my life. Know right where everything is."

"Let's go back upstairs and check on Peggy. I'll need to see the toolbox you keep up there as well. Everything seems fine down here."

"Don't keep no tools upstairs, Sheriff. If I need any, I just run down here and get them from the set we keep under the counter. That way, I can pick up any new parts I need from down here while I'm at it."

Dalton checked the toolbox under the counter, but nothing seemed to be missing. The old saw in the bottom of the wooden case didn't have any signs of blood, and all of the saws on the wall still had their clean, never used look. But, he'd better have the crime lab team examine them, just in case.

They re-entered the living room to find Peggy still sitting on the couch, sobbing into what was left of the tissue. Mark went over, sat beside her, placed his arm around her shoulder, and hugged her to him as they both rocked back and forth.

"Peggy, Mark said there wasn't much money in the cash register, only enough to start the day. Do you have access to the business account or the family account?"

"No. Like I said, Jack took care of everything. Always has, since our parents died. I've been after Mark to learn more about running the store, but Jack said he didn't seem to have the patience to listen. Mark doesn't always listen to me either, even when I tell him something for his own good."

Mark ducked his head. "I'm sorry, Sis. Guess I should have tried harder."

"It's too late to worry about that now. I don't know what we're going to do. Jack kept a little bit of money up here. That will keep us going for a few days. I suppose we'll have to sell the store, if neither of us can run it. I just don't know where to turn."

Peggy rubbed her forehead.

"Headache back, Sis?"

"Worse than ever. I feel sick. I'm afraid you'll have to excuse me, Joe." She made a dash for the hall door.

Mark stood uncomfortably in the doorway, listening to the sounds coming from the bathroom. Dalton walked over to the mantle and examined a grouping of family portraits. There was a photo of Peggy sitting on her father's lap, but none of Mark. Maybe his mother hadn't gotten around to framing any pictures of him before her death? The rest of the photographs were of Jack, from birth to his final football game. Mrs. Hatfield hadn't lived to see her son graduate.

Dalton picked up the one that featured himself and Jack riding on the shoulders of their teammates at the end of that championship game, a day none of them would ever forget. How quickly lives can turn from triumph to tragedy.

Thoughts chased each other inside Dalton's head like squirrels circling around a tree trunk, so fast he couldn't keep up. Jack should have realized he wasn't a man of steel, wasn't invincible, wouldn't last forever. What if he hadn't made any arrangements for his family in case something happened to him? Or at least appointed someone to watch over their affairs? What would happen to them?

Mark was about as sharp as a bowling ball. He'd dropped out of high school as soon as he'd gotten his license and worked as a delivery boy for his brother and the other downtown merchants. As far as Dalton could recall, Peggy hadn't finished high school either. After their parents' deaths, she'd become reclusive, preferring to stay home and keep house for her brothers. He doubted she knew a socket wrench from a pair of pliers.

The sound of the toilet flushing brought both men into the hallway. Peggy headed straight for her bedroom. Dalton and Mark followed her. Mark straightened the sheets and tucked the faded yellow quilt around her.

"My grandmother made this for me when I was a little girl. I wish she'd still been alive when we needed her all those years ago." Peggy fingered the ragged hem of the quilt.

"When Daddy killed Mother, he pretty much destroyed any chance we ever had of leading normal lives. We were all too busy just trying to survive afterwards. I've never forgiven him for that. Jack tried to take over for our parents, but that was a big mistake. We should have learned how to fend for ourselves."

Peggy turned and looked up at Dalton.

"I've never had a job. I have no experience, no education and yet I have to find some way to take care of us. Mark can keep making deliveries, but that won't begin to cover expenses."

Mark shook his head, obviously at a loss for words.

"I can't even seem to think about making arrangements for Jack's funeral. My brain feels like a block of ice. What if we don't have enough money to bury him? I suppose we could sell Mother's dishes. Miss Mamie said they're worth a lot."

"I wouldn't make any quick decisions about your future, Peggy. You should probably contact a lawyer as soon as possible," Dalton responded. "That new young fella just opened his practice across the street from my office. Word at the courthouse square is that he's smart, eager, and reasonable. I'll bet he can help you get Jack's affairs in order. Maybe even find someone to help you run the store. He can check to see if Jack had insurance, things like that."

Peggy began to sob softly again.

"You can also call my office if you need anything. I'll do my best to help out."

"Thanks, Sheriff. Sis and I appreciate that. Soon as she's up to it, we'll contact that lawyer."

Dalton didn't have any more questions. They obviously needed time alone to deal with the shock, and he wanted to get away from their grief, get outside where he could breathe. He mumbled another brief condolence, promised again to get in touch as soon as he had any news, and headed toward the back door.

Outside on the landing Dalton heaved a sigh of relief and glanced at the damp sky. He hadn't felt this useless since his wife had gone into labor with their first child.

Dalton clanged down the metal stairs and started back to his office.

Unless she was very good at faking shock, which he doubted, Peggy was genuinely surprised to hear about the decapitation. Mark was more of a mystery. His face had been much harder to read, but Dalton hadn't detected any guilt there. Anger, possibly, over his brother's murder?

Dalton jaywalked across Market Street, wondering again how the Hatfield's would manage without their big brother.

CHAPTER 5

Dalton paused for a fraction of a second at the intersection before crossing. The sound of screeching tires brought him up short. He waved an apology at the mayor and jogged back around to the driver's door. Might as well fill His Honor in right now since there wasn't any traffic behind him waiting to cross the intersection.

"Mornin', Buck."

"Morning, Joe. My secretary paged me about Jack Hatfield." The mayor shifted his car into park. "I was over in Paducah, breakfast meeting with Mayor Hosman about getting that new canine unit for you. Couldn't believe it. I figured I'd better dash back to the office and see what I could do to help you out. What have we got so far?"

Canine unit? He'd asked for one two years ago, and now Buck was suddenly acting on it? Wonderful how an election year could move your requests from bottom to top of the mayor's "to do" list. Dalton leaned his arm against the roof of the car and lowered his head.

"Jeffords says Jack was strangled. His head was cut off, and his body was slung over the arm of the Superman statue. He should be back late this afternoon with a preliminary autopsy report. I'll meet with the media then."

The mayor shook his balding head. "Better let me handle the media. I remember how much you hated public speaking class in high school."

Dalton still hated speaking in public, but no way was he going to let the mayor step in and do his job for him.

"Won't be necessary, Buck. My staff has already set the meeting up for later today at my office. Besides, I got used to handling the media a couple of elections back."

The mayor didn't look convinced.

"I presume you've spoken to Jack's family? As if they haven't had enough to deal with already."

"Yeah, I thought it might be a little easier coming from me. Not that anything makes news like that any easier."

The mayor paused and looked through the windshield wipers moving slowly back and forth. "Seems like only yesterday that I was still the principal at Metropolis Community and you two were either playing football or playing pranks on your teachers. You still hold the record for most time spent in detention."

It didn't seem that long ago to Dalton either, even though both of his children had already graduated from high school.

"While driving back here all I could think about was that final game. Jack could easily have been an all-pro star. Could've put this town on the map. Instead, he just let it all slip away. Settled for small town life."

Dalton wasn't about to let that statement pass unchallenged.

"Wasn't exactly his fault Buck. When his parents died, Jack felt he had no choice but to take over the business, and raise the two younger kids. There just wasn't anybody else to do it."

"I suppose you're right, but what a loss to the sporting world."

The mayor looked up at Dalton. "It's going to be pretty tough on you investigating the death of a close friend. Think you can handle a case this big? The entire county is going to be screaming for answers. We should be able to get the state police or the FBI to help out if your office needs it."

The fact that his former high school principal couldn't seem to adjust to the idea that the juvenile delinquent who so often languished in detention was now the chief law enforcement officer of Massac County frequently irritated Dalton. Maybe he should start carrying his high school diploma in his wallet.

"We'll handle it just fine, Buck. I'll let you know if we need any help."

Dalton shifted to his other foot and looked at the ground. The weight in his gut seemed to be getting heavier by the minute.

"You know, Buck, Jack's worn that Superman costume to every major social event since the team gave it to him, but I sure never thought he'd die in it."

"Neither did I. I can't imagine why anyone would kill him. Jack didn't have an enemy in the world. And why hang him over the arm of the statue? Have you given any thought to that? It would have been much simpler to bury a body in the woods or dump it in the river."

A car pulled up behind the mayor at the intersection and waited.

"Of course I've thought about it," Dalton said. "The killer took a big chance, which makes me think it was probably a local who knows that Market Street has less traffic than the cemetery after dark. Besides, most murder victims are killed by someone they know, not strangers."

"True, but you can't afford to overlook any possibilities. So, you have no leads and no witnesses? Doesn't sound too promising."

The driver behind them honked, and Dalton waved her around.

"Big Ed was on Grace Lipinski's steps at least part of the night. I doubt if he'll be of much help, though; he was way past three sheets to the wind."

"Big Ed hasn't drawn a sober breath as long as anyone can remember," the mayor agreed.

"One of my deputies is filling him with black coffee right now. I'll see what I can get out of him when I get back to the detention center."

"I'd better let you get at it then. I'll be in my office if you need anything. You've got to solve this one quickly, Joe. The whole town is going to be in a panic. I'll be happy to advise you on this. Just come by my office any time."

Dalton nodded. Actually, he'd just as soon visit a proctologist as visit Buck's office and ask for advice on a case. Buck had been an excellent high school principal, and was a passable mayor, but he was certainly no trained investigator.

The mayor steered toward his office. Dalton checked for traffic, crossed the street again, and walked to the end of the block.

He pushed his way through the heavy glass door and stepped inside the detention center's stark reception area. It seemed like weeks instead of hours since he'd gone outside to retrieve Big Ed from Mrs. Lipinski's stairwell. Behind the bulletproof glass, George Means responded to the code the sheriff gave and unlocked the door to the area Dalton indicated.

"Did Doody get a statement from Big Ed?" Dalton asked the dispatcher.

"Not yet. Big Ed has spent most of the morning in the bathroom. Doody's still filling him up with coffee."

Dalton headed down the narrow hallway toward his office. He believed in running a very tight ship. The Massac County Detention Center was as clean as a whistle and prisoners were treated well, but this was no country club facility where inmates could bask in the frills. Dalton did all he could to discourage returnees.

Big Ed was seated in a chair in Dalton's private office still fighting a bad case of the shakes. Whether they were caused from being drunk or from being on the scene during the discovery of Jack Hatfield's body was anybody's guess. Means came into the office on Dalton's heels.

"I'll take care of Big Ed, George. You can go back to work."

Means stalked off to his desk, muttering loud enough to be heard.

Dalton sat down at his desk, and Doody Jenson scooted up a chair and reached for his notebook.

"Just tell us whatever you remember about last night, Big Ed, no matter how small or unimportant it might seem to you."

"When I woke up from my afternoon nap, I was so thirsty I had to hike over to Pete's Place right then," Big Ed began.

"Thought I might be able to find a generous soul to hoist a few with. I got lucky and met somebody from the Riverboat casino, a tourist with more money than sense. I told him some of my old courtroom stories, and he bought me a few drinks." Big Ed paused for another sip of the strong coffee.

"Do you remember his name?"

"No. We never formally introduced ourselves."

"How long were you at Pete's Place?" Dalton asked.

"All afternoon and most of the evening. That guy bought me enough booze to last me a while. Guess I should've saved some." He shook his head sadly.

"What time did you leave?"

"I'm not sure. It was way before closing, though. When the drinks ran out, I was feeling pretty comfortable and thought I would make it an early evening for once." Big Ed shivered and held his cup out to Doody Jenson for a refill.

"But you didn't make it home, did you?"

"By the time I reached Market Street, I was way too cold and tired to make it the rest of the way. So I sat down in old lady Lipinski's doorway, on those steps there, to rest for a few minutes. I must've fallen asleep for some time in spite of the wind. You know she threw a shoe at me. Maybe I should charge her with assault." Big Ed warmed his hands on the newly filled cup.

Dalton ignored Big Ed's last comment. "Did you see or hear anyone else besides Jack at the statue?"

"No. And I only noticed the body on the statue when I heard you bang the door and you woke me up. I saw it when I looked around to see where I was. You know, Sheriff, you guys really ought to fix that door. It's loud enough to wake the dead."

Dalton wasn't amused by the pun. Big Ed wiped off a sheepish grin and continued.

"I didn't realize Hatfield was dead until I saw your cup hit the ground. Haven't seen you move that fast since high school."

Big Ed's face suddenly changed colors, and Dalton pointed toward the nearest bathroom.

Dalton turned to his deputy.

"When Big Ed comes back, have him read and sign his statement, then drive him home. He isn't going to be much use today. We'll try again later."

"Sure thing, Sheriff."

"He doesn't live far, but he's in no shape to make it by himself. George can direct you if Big Ed can't."

Doody left Dalton's office just as Wilson entered.

"I caught Ruby on her way out the door, headed to work," he told Dalton. "She didn't turn on her television this morning, so she hadn't heard about the murder. She was pretty shaken up, and I had to wait for her to calm down long enough to question her."

Wilson glanced down at his notes. "According to Ruby, Hatfield called her at work yesterday to tell her that he had an unexpected late meeting with a salesman, and he'd have to cancel their plans for dinner. She hadn't seen or heard from

43

him since. She said she'd had a long day so she decided to spend the evening at home, relaxing."

At least the part about Jack meeting with the salesman tallied with what Mark and Peggy had told him.

"Did she see or talk to anyone else?" Dalton asked.

"Nope. She says she was home alone all night. No one visited her, and she had no phone calls. She said she had no idea who would want to kill him. Said everyone who knew Hatfield loved him."

The deputy looked up from his notes. "She seemed pretty shocked by the whole thing. She went to pieces before I left, and I asked a neighbor to come over and stay with her. My guess is your dentist is going to need a substitute receptionist for the next few days."

"Ruby trusts you, so I want you to check her out closely," Dalton said. "Find out who she hangs around with. Jack's family mentioned that he and Ruby hadn't been seeing much of each other lately. It's possible they'd had some sort of falling out. I don't think she did it, but we can't rule her out yet. If she did do it, she'd have needed help getting his body on the statue."

"I'll see what I can come up with."

Wilson tossed the report on Dalton's desk and headed toward the door.

"Going to lunch. Want me to bring you anything?"

"No thanks," Dalton replied. "I'll get something later." When he could bring himself to face a plate full of food.

CHAPTER 6

Deputy Linda Peters rapped her nightstick on Miss Mamie Timsley's door. Deputy Craig Edwards leaned against the stair railing and chewed on a toothpick not much wider than he was.

Linda's face reflected back at her from the door glass. Good thing she usually wore her hair in a ponytail to work. Her bangs seemed to have been blown everywhere but across her forehead. And the dryer must be shrinking her uniforms again. Her shirt buttons always seemed to be in a bind, and the pants zipper was getting much harder to close.

At least the ancient awning was keeping the cold, autumnal rain from soaking them, assuming the wind didn't rip it off.

The door creaked open, and Miss Mamie's face lit up at the prospect of unexpected visitors.

"You young folks come inside and out of the cold."

"Thank you, ma'am," Linda responded, stepping into the oven-like apartment.

Miss Mamie flitted around her kitchen tempting the deputies with offerings of food until they were forced to give in.

"A cup of tea will warm the two of you right up. Then we can talk."

Linda watched as Miss Mamie filled her old kettle with fresh water and set it on the stove. Then the elderly woman ushered both deputies toward the nearby chairs.

Linda had a daughter and had been to many tea parties. Craig had only been blessed with boys, so she knew his experience with such niceties was next to nil. He would likely be hard put not to break a delicate cup or drop cookie crumbs on the floor.

Linda sat down, adjusted her gun belt, and glanced around the apartment. The afghan spread across the back softened the old couch, making it look almost comfortable and homey. Crocheted doilies covered the rickety end tables, their lacy designs helping hide some of the scratched wood.

While the kettle heated on the tiny stove, Miss Mamie got out her best teapot and cups and began to set the table.

"Don't get much company any more. Most of my old friends have passed on."

She fished around in the cabinet next to the stove, came up with a bag of cookies, took them out of the plastic tray, and placed them on a lovely, slightly chipped china plate.

"You wouldn't think it to look at me now, but I used to be a cook on a towboat. I was just a young 'un when my mamma and papa drowned in the flood of thirty-seven. Cooking was the only thing she had managed to teach me. I never married. Never felt the need to. I was kept plenty busy feeding those hungry deck hands."

Miss Mamie placed the cookie plate at Craig's elbow and favored him with a full-dentured smile.

"When I retired, I came here to live. They call it an efficiency apartment because everything is in one room. Efficient maybe, but there's hardly enough room in here to cuss a cat." Miss Mamie cackled at her own wit.

"It's near the river, and that makes me feel at home. I can hear the towboats signaling each other."

Miss Mamie poured the hot water into the teapot and spooned in some loose tea.

"Such a shame about Jack. I heard about it on the news this morning, but I still can't believe it. Who would do something like that? Have you caught him yet?"

"No, ma'am, not yet. We're still investigating," Linda responded. "That's why we're here. We'd like to ask you a few questions, if we may. Can you see into the Hatfield's apartment from your front window?"

"'Course I can. I keep a close eye on that family," she admitted. "I can see the whole living room and most of the dining room. I really don't–didn't—see Jack all that often, but Mark and Peggy sit in the living room every evening and watch television after supper."

Miss Mamie sat down opposite Craig. She nodded toward the ancient television near her couch.

"I don't watch it much myself. Nothing fit for decent folks on that old set these days."

She pushed her thick glasses higher on her nose and peered at each deputy. Her thin, white hair stood out like a halo around her face.

"Did you happen to look across to the Hatfield's windows last night, Miss Mamie?" Linda balanced her cup on her knee while she reached for another Fig Newton.

"Yes, I looked over there several times. I saw Mark in the living room by himself. He's a little 'backward' as my mamma would have said. He never goes out at night, just sits there and watches the television."

The elderly woman chewed thoughtfully.

"I didn't see Peggy. She must have gone to bed early with one of her headaches. She suffers from migraines, you know. Not many people know Mark or Peggy well, but I've lived here a long time, and I've gotten to know all of them. Such a shame. That family's had so much to deal with, with their parents and that whole situation. And now this." Miss Mamie sighed and shook her head at the tragedies that had befallen poor Mark and Peggy.

"Did you see Jack at all last night, Miss Mamie?" Linda inquired while Craig carefully set his half-full cup back on the table.

"Let me think. No, I don't rightly remember seeing Jack. Every time I looked over there, it was just poor Mark sitting by himself."

Miss Mamie spooned enough sugar into her tea to make Linda cringe.

"Jack was such a nice boy, taking care of his brother and sister all those years. How will they manage without him? I really don't see how they'll ever be able to run that store by themselves. If I could get around a mite better, I'd help out."

"Did you see anyone at all on the street last night, Miss Mamie?" Linda asked.

"I hardly ever look down there after dark. There's really nothing to see. You wouldn't believe how lonely and deserted Market Street is at night." She took a sip of her tea.

"Did you hear anything unusual?"

"Unusual, no, I don't think so. Just Big Ed singing at the top of his lungs down the street. He does that a lot. A body gets used to it after a while."

"What time did you hear Big Ed singing?" Craig asked.

"I'm not sure. I went to bed around midnight and fell right off to sleep. His awful caterwauling woke me up sometime later, but I don't know exactly when that was." She stared at the deputies in obvious disapproval of Big Ed's late activities.

Linda exchanged a glance with Craig and then took a quick gulp of tea to hide a grin.

"We'll mention it to Sheriff Dalton, ma'am. Perhaps a word from him might convince Big Ed to be a little quieter when he's in the neighborhood," she responded setting her cup down.

"Are you aware of any enemies Jack might have had, Miss Mamie? Do you know any reason why someone would have wanted to hurt him?"

"Mercy, no. Jack was one of the most respected men in this town. I can't imagine anyone wanting to hurt him. I can't bear to think what this will do to Mark and Peggy. I really must go over there and see if there's something I can do for them."

Miss Mamie turned to Craig. "More tea, young man?"

"No thank you, ma'am. If you don't mind, we'll just be on our way. We have some other interviews to conduct."

Linda handed Miss Mamie the department's business card and urged her to call if she remembered any new information.

A canvas of the other nearby apartments produced no new information. No one else appeared to have seen or heard anything the night before, except for the common complaint about Big Ed's singing.

"That just leaves Mrs. Lipinski to interview," Linda said to Craig. They had purposely left the owner of the appliance store for last. Her apartment was nearest the detention center and the crime scene.

"Just so long as we don't have to attend another tea party," Craig commented. "She could have at least had some Oreos instead of those stale Fig Newtons."

"It could have been worse." Linda continued as Craig stared at her, "She could have made you stick your pinkie out when you were sipping your tea."

Craig snorted as they continued down the block.

CHAPTER 7

Grace Lipinski carefully checked the identification of both deputies before allowing them in. She walked slowly across her living room with the help of a cane and eased her arthritic body into a chair by the fireplace. Linda took a seat on the couch, as thankful as Craig that Mrs. Lipinski hadn't offered them anything to eat or drink. Craig stood near the front window, pen and notebook at the ready.

"Mrs. Lipinski, you called our office early this morning about a disturbance. Could you please tell us about that?"

"You bet I can, young lady. Mr. Big Ed Simmons was lolling on my stairwell, singing so loudly I could not get a wink of sleep. I hope you lock him up and throw away the key."

"And at what time did this happen?"

"It was well after midnight when I called your office the first time, close to one o'clock. No one came. I am just relieved that he did not try to murder me, or worse. You people certainly did not seem concerned." She glared at the two deputies.

"Big Ed has never been a threat to anyone but himself, but I do apologize for the delay, ma'am. We were very short handed last night. Two of the deputies were off sick, and there was a big accident near Golconda that we had to respond to."

Craig spoke up, helping Linda defend Sheriff Dalton. "Otherwise we would have responded much sooner. Are you sure

50

Big Ed wasn't on your steps earlier in the evening?"

The elderly woman took a tissue out of her sweater pocket and wiped her mouth.

"If he was, I didn't hear him. Only heard him after midnight. When you people didn't show up, I threw an old shoe down at him, and he got quiet for a while. I thought he had gone home."

She dabbed at her eyes with the tissue. "When he started up again, I dialed nine-one-one, and that time the sheriff came. Good thing he did, or I might have had to take matters into my own hands; a person can only stand so much, after all."

Craig peeled himself off the windowsill. "The dispatcher told the sheriff that you threatened to shoot Mr. Simmons if he didn't quieten down. I'm afraid we'll have to see the weapon and your firearm owner identification, ma'am."

"I do not have any owner identification because I do not keep any firearms. I just said that to get the sheriff off his rump and over here. I figured that comment would get someone's attention. Good thing I called, too—now you can put that murderer in prison where he belongs."

Linda spoke up. "You think Big Ed Simmons murdered Jack Hatfield, Mrs. Lipinski? Did you see them together downstairs last night? Did you hear or see anything that might tie him to this case?"

Mrs. Lipinski busied herself plumping the pillows behind her back.

"No, I didn't see or hear them down there, but Big Ed Simmons is just a good-for-nothing, freeloading drunk. My daughter says he brings old junk into our store all the time. Tries to get her to buy it so he'll have drink money. He does that with all the other stores on Market Street as well. It is only a matter of time before he kills someone, if he has not already."

She sniffed and rubbed her gnarled hands together. "You

mark my words, Big Ed Simmons was after Jack Hatfield for drink money, and when he didn't get it, he killed Jack. It is just a thousand wonders he didn't break in here and murder me, for all you people care."

"You have our word, ma'am, that if we find any evidence linking Big Ed to Jack Hatfield's death, he will be arrested and charged," Craig said.

"Humph, I certainly hope so. Market Street is not even safe any more. Drunks sleeping all over the place, a fine young man killed practically on my doorstep. You'd better lock that old drunk up before he does worse." The old lady pulled her sweater tightly around her thin shoulders.

"Did you see Jack Hatfield's body on the statue, ma'am?" Linda asked.

"No, it was still dark, and I was too busy trying to defend myself from Big Ed Simmons. When I saw the sheriff walk up to my steps, I figured he would arrest that criminal, so I went back to bed. I did not know about poor Jack Hatfield's death until I got up to go to the bathroom a little later and saw all the activity down on the street." She wiped at a tear that Linda suspected didn't exist.

"Jack Hatfield was a lovely boy. Trust that disgusting drunk to do something outrageous like hanging his body on the statue. My poor, dear John must be turning in his grave at what this town has become."

Linda changed the subject, guessing that Mrs. Lipinski didn't have any further information. A little community relations might help keep her from harassing the sheriff over Big Ed.

"I remember your husband. We bought our first washing machine from him when we moved into our house. You must have lived here a long time."

"John and I opened this store some fifty years ago. We had the first television set ever seen in Metropolis. We could only get one channel, and they only broadcasted at night. Folks used to sit on their car hoods and watch it through the store window. And let me tell you, young lady, Market Street was safe from the likes of Big Ed Simmons in those days."

Linda stood and handed her the department's business card, fearing she might dial nine-one-one again without it.

"We have to get back to our office and file this report. If you think of anything at all that might help us, Mrs. Lipinski, please call. We appreciate the information you've given us."

Craig followed her to the door. "Please, don't bother getting up; we'll see ourselves out."

"I hope you keep Big Ed Simmons in jail. I won't sleep a wink unless you do."

On the way back to the detention center Craig ventured an opinion.

"Bet that gun she doesn't own was stashed in the magazine basket beside her chair."

"I never bet against a sure thing. I just hope she never tries to fire it. With those crippled hands, she'd likely take out half the block."

CHAPTER 8

Dalton choked down a gulp of late afternoon coffee and glanced at the box of donuts Peters had brought with her earlier that morning. Maybe just one, to tide him over until supper? He was hungry and tired, and, so far the investigation hadn't unearthed many clues.

He was reaching for a cinnamon glazed when Means stuck his head in the door without knocking—as usual—and announced the coroner.

"Call the deputies in, George. I want them to hear this."

Jeffords stepped into the office and looked pointedly at the coffee maker.

"Help yourself," Dalton offered, "But you drink it at your own risk."

"Thanks. If it's hot, maybe it'll at least take the chill off me."

As Jeffords sipped his coffee and waited for his laptop to finish booting up on Dalton's desk, the deputies filed in and took seats.

When they were all there, Jeffords began. "According to the pathologist, Hatfield ate about an hour before his death. He died around nine last night, give or take. His head was cut off with either a sharp saw or hatchet-like weapon."

Jeffords demonstrated on himself with his finger. "The cut was fairly clean and straight, but you can still see a mark on

Hatfield's neck indicating that he was strangled with an electrical cord common to most small appliances."

The coroner clicked on a file, waited for the pictures from his digital camera to load, and began scrolling slowly through them.

A picture of Jack Hatfield's severed head appeared on the screen. Doody Jenson dropped his donut into the wastebasket. Peters, Edwards, and Wilson all stared at the computer. Dalton felt his teeth clinch together.

"What had he eaten?" Peters asked. "If it was restaurant food, maybe we could track it down."

"Steak and vegetables, according to the pathologist. With so many restaurants here and over in Paducah, it's going to be a tough job narrowing down where he ate that meal. Not to mention the possibility of someone grilling out in their garage or something."

"Mark Hatfield said a tool salesman offered to buy Jack's dinner if he'd meet him after store hours. Doody, when you've finished checking out all the local eating places, start on Paducah," Dalton said.

Jenson nodded and excused himself from the meeting, indicating a sudden need for the bathroom.

A picture of Hatfield's body hanging over the arm of the statue scrolled into view. Dalton wondered if he'd ever be able to get that sight out of his mind.

"I'd wager the decapitation was done somewhere else, and the body was then wrapped in plastic and brought to the statue. Or if it was done there it had to be right underneath where you found most of the blood," Jeffords said.

"I don't see the killer spending that much time with the body out in the open. Too much risk," Dalton commented.

"Neither do I," Wilson chimed in.

"Since Hatfield was already dead, the blood didn't spurt, but oozed slowly into a puddle under his body. As you can see in the photos, there isn't much sign of a struggle, no defensive wounds," Jeffords continued.

"Meaning the killer did take Jack by surprise and strangled him from behind," Dalton said. "You think it's likely the killer was someone Hatfield knew, someone he wasn't afraid to turn his back on?"

"Yeah. Like you said before, Hatfield was too strong to let anyone take him down head on without putting up a massive defense."

The coroner scrolled to the next picture, Hatfield's naked torso on the pathologist's table. Dalton felt his fingers lock onto his chair arms.

"Notice the way the blood pooled under the skin on his back? He must've fallen backwards and lain there for a while," Jeffords said.

"How long had he been dead before his body was moved?" Dalton asked.

"About thirty minutes, not much longer."

Dalton sat rigid while the coroner scrolled through a few more pictures and gave a blow-by-blow account of the autopsy. In all of his years as sheriff, he'd never had to deal with a situation like this.

"Toxicology reports will be ready in a week or so. Then we'll know if the blood on the ladder was Hatfield's, the killer's, or maybe both. It'll take at least a month to get the report on the slides made from sections of Hatfield's vital organs. I doubt if that will turn up anything, though. I'll let you know when the rest of the reports come in."

Jeffords began shutting down the computer. Dalton mopped his sweaty brow with a Kleenex yanked from a nearby box. Wouldn't do for anyone to check his blood pressure at the moment; he doubted any existing apparatus could register that high. When he determined who had killed his old friend, somebody had better be nearby to hold him back.

"Did you find the list of tool salesmen I left on your desk?" Dalton asked Peters.

"Yes, sir."

"Divide it up with Edwards and contact them. Find out who Jack met last night."

"Yes, sir."

"Wilson, anything on Ruby Miller's friends yet?"

"No, sir."

"Stay on it and keep me up to date."

Wilson nodded, and the deputies headed out to their assignments. The coroner gathered up his equipment.

Dalton tapped his thumbs together for several seconds, deep in thought. The intercom buzzed, and he punched the button. "Yes, George?"

"Several reporters here to see you, Sheriff. I put them in the interview room."

"Thanks, George. We'll be there shortly."

Dalton turned to the coroner. "Have you talked to Mark or Peggy yet about releasing the body?"

"Yeah, I spoke to Mark. Apparently Peggy isn't up to making any decisions today. I'm sure Jack hadn't made any prior arrangements with our funeral home. Like most people, he probably thought he could postpone the inevitable by not making any plans for it." Jeffords raised an eyebrow at Dalton.

"Ginger handles all of that stuff. I know we have a will, but I don't know if she's been in to see you. I'll check it out." In a decade or so.

"Mark asked me to handle the arrangements. Don't think he has much of a head for this kind of thing. I'll take care of it and cut them as much slack as I possibly can. He didn't seem to know whether or not there was any insurance."

"I'd appreciate it if you would help them. Let me know if there is something I can do to help out. What about the crowd at the funeral?"

"I've been thinking about that," Jeffords responded. "Since the whole town knew Jack, most residents will want to show up and pay their respects. And there will be plenty of others attending out of plain, old-fashioned curiosity."

"True," Dalton said. "Not many victims are decapitated in this town, guns generally being the weapon of choice. The entire county is likely to turn out."

"Jeffords and McCann is a fairly spacious old place, but I'm not sure it's big enough to hold what promises to be the biggest funeral in Metropolis's history. It'll take some careful planning just for seating arrangements. Flowers will be a whole 'nother problem."

The coroner grabbed his jacket off the back of the chair. "Wonder if the murderer will have the nerve to show up at the funeral. If the killer knew Hatfield, he'll have to be there or his absence will arouse suspicion."

"Exactly. And I'll be there watching for anything suspicious. Guess we'd better speak to the ladies and gentlemen of the press."

Jeffords rubbed his stomach. "After we talk to them, I think I'll head over to Cubby's and pick up a pizza. My wife gets cranky when she's hungry, and she's been holding down the fort for me all day."

CHAPTER 9

The deputies left shortly after the coroner, but it was long after his workday usually ended before Dalton was able to sink wearily behind the wheel of his official car, struggle into the seat belt, and head for home. Fielding phone calls from anxious local officials and plowing through a mound of paperwork had kept him tied to his desk far longer than usual; and he'd barely made a dent in the pile. At least he didn't have to scrunch like a sardine in this car the way he did in his wife's little foreign piece of tin.

Dalton turned on the windshield wipers. A steady rain had been falling most of the day. The clouds behind the courthouse were getting heavier by the minute, and he hoped to get home before the real downpour. He glanced again at the statue through his rearview mirror as he turned down Market Street. With the body removed and the blood washed away, Superman looked like his usual, dignified self. Dalton made a couple of quick turns and headed down Fifth Street.

He felt his stomach tighten with hunger as he passed the Dairy Queen. He'd missed lunch—hadn't really thought about it—and now his insides were reminding him of this fact. Should've had another of those donuts. He could almost taste the DQ burgers. He figured he'd better go on home and pray that his wife wasn't starting him on yet another diet.

Dalton knew that Ginger worried about him every time he

walked out the front door, just like all other law enforcement wives; but rather than fuss about the dangers of the job she focused on his weight. He often came home to low-fat meals, which he bragged about publicly, but privately thought tasted like cardboard; he preferred meals that swam in grease. Unfortunately, his metabolism had gone to sleep some time in his late thirties, and what was once muscle was now dissolving into fat.

He parked in front of the old, brick, two-story home on the corner of Catherine Street and started up the walk. Bright lights shined through every window. Ginger had an aversion to dark rooms, and he figured that the resulting light bill probably kept the power company in business. A huge porch, partially screened-in, surrounded two sides of the house. Ginger had been after him to cover the furniture out there before the weather damaged it. Maybe he'd get to it this weekend.

He opened the front door and found himself quickly enveloped in a bear hug. He was also met with the smell of his favorite meal—meatloaf with catsup burned on top. The aroma grabbed his nostrils and brought a grin to his big face.

Dalton gave Ginger a wet kiss, struggled out of his jacket and gun belt, and slung them over the hall tree.

"I heard about Jack's death when I went to the Planet to turn in my column this morning," his wife said. "The entire newspaper was abuzz with the story. I figured you'd need a substantial meal after the day you've had. So do I, for that matter. You're not going to believe what happened."

Dalton put his arm around Ginger's shoulders, and they walked together through the living room and dining room and into the large, high-ceilinged kitchen. Its yellow walls gave the room a sunny look even on dark days like this one.

He heaved a sigh. "I tried to call you about Jack, but every time I had a free minute, you weren't home. Hope I never have another day like this one. Tell me about your day first."

He plopped down at the old oak table, rescued at a garage

sale and lovingly restored. His wife had re-designed the kitchen to look like the original owner still cooked there, with the dishwasher and other modern appliances carefully hidden behind cabinet doors. He watched with pleasure as she served up his favorite meat and vegetables from the antique wood-burning stove that had been converted to gas.

"When I got to the Planet office this morning, the reception desk was deserted," she began. "Ditto the managing editor's desk. In fact the entire newspaper staff seemed to be missing. I was about to dial nine-one-one and report a mass kidnapping when I saw the back door standing open."

She placed a heaping plate in front of him and returned to the stove.

"I looked outside and there they all stood, gawking over the fence, trying to see what was going on a half a block away at the statue. No one seemed to mind the fact that the post office building was entirely blocking their view."

Ginger sat down, and they both began shoveling into the meal like prisoners who had been on bread and water for a week. Dalton marveled that she could eat so much and never gain an extra pound.

She was as small and pretty as when he'd first noticed her in biology class in high school. The only difference was the few gray hairs mixed in with the dark red that was so suggestive of her name. Well, he had a couple of gray hairs too, and he still found her as exciting as when they had first married.

"The staff told me about Jack's murder. It made me sick. I was about to drop my column on Ken's desk and leave when he returned from covering the story and asked how I'd like to move up in the world of journalism."

"Move up how?" Dalton said, talking and chewing at the same time.

"To the job of feature editor. Just temporarily, of course. Ken Davidson is totally livid that Marty Hoggs chose this particular time to go goose hunting in some unknown part of Canada."

"Does he really think Hoggsey should have known that there'd be a sensational murder while he was away? Pass the salt, please."

"The problem is, Marty didn't bother to leave a number where he could be reached because, as he put it, 'Nothing more exciting than a tractor pull ever happens in Metropolis in the fall.' Ken wants to teach him a lesson by letting someone else do the job of writing feature stories while he's gone."

Dalton put the saltshaker down. "That's great. You deserve to move up."

"I spoke to Mark on the phone, interviewed a couple of the regular hardware store customers and a few of Jack's neighbors. Miss Mamie even plied me with cookies and tea. I turned in my article and made it home just in time to fix a meal guaranteed to give us both higher cholesterol."

He reached for another slice of bread. "You don't seem too excited about this. I thought you were hoping for the chance to break out of the gardening section and see your byline on the front page. This is certainly big news."

"I've been dying to show Ken what I can do. It just never occurred to me that the chance would come because of the murder of someone I knew. Particularly a murder this gruesome." She shuddered slightly at the thought.

"I'm just thankful that Ken is personally handling the investigative reporting end of this and I'm just writing about Jack's life."

"I thought you'd enjoy getting involved in an investigation. You always want to hear every detail of mine."

"Talking to Mark was really hard. He seems so lost. I don't know when I've ever felt so sorry for anyone. How was Peggy handling the news when you saw her?"

Dalton buttered his slice of bread and described his visit to the Hatfields' for his wife.

"I have to investigate them as suspects. Fortunately, Mark

seems to have an alibi, and I don't think Peggy could've done it without help, so that leaves them out." He mopped his greasy plate with the bread.

"Okay, but who does that leave?"

"Jack met with a salesman last night. We can't seem to locate him. And things apparently weren't going quite as smoothly between Jack and Ruby as everyone thought. And I still have to consider the possibility of a random killer."

"Not a lot of good choices. I just pray the killer isn't someone we know."

Ginger gathered up the leftovers while he loaded the dishwasher. That job done, Dalton flopped onto the wide, firm couch avoiding the rather delicate chairs by the fireplace. His clothes were still slightly damp, this time from the trip home, but he was far too comfortable in front of the warm fire to even consider going upstairs to change.

He told Ginger everything else he knew about the case while the rain, blown around by the wind, rat-tat-tatted against the windows. They discussed what he'd learned from the forensic pathologist's preliminary report, and the bloodstained ladder Deputy Wilson had found.

Dalton had noticed it took two deputies making a trip around the courthouse to come up with the ladder, but had not, as yet, dealt with that. He'd keep an eye on Doody and Wilson for a while to see if they needed any prodding from him.

"Why would someone kill Jack like that?" Ginger's hair brushed her cheek as she shook her head in disbelief. "Could it have been a robbery? Maybe he interrupted someone breaking into the store when he returned home?"

"No, I don't think so," Dalton replied. "But the thought did cross my mind." He reached over and touched her hair.

"If that was the case, the killer would've left Jack's body there. Or dumped it somewhere in the hope that we wouldn't find it for some time. Leaving it on the statue like that was a message of some kind. The killer wanted us to find him there, where there was no chance we'd miss it."

He neglected to tell her how he had missed it at first.

"My gut says Jack had an enemy, hard as I find that to believe. I just have to figure out who it was."

He reached for the remote, ready to stop discussing the murder.

"It could have been random. If it was, there could be more murders, right? But I agree with you that it's more likely an enemy." Ginger said. "Either way, you've got a tough job. Whoever killed Jack has to be found and stopped."

"And the sooner the better."

The murder of his old high school buddy had really shaken Dalton; it had brought home thoughts of his own mortality. No use burdening Ginger with that. Or the fact that the usual pressure to catch and convict without making a dumb mistake and freeing the perp would be far heavier in this case than in any other he'd ever faced. He just hoped he could solve this murder quickly.

CHAPTER 10

Later, Ginger suggested they go to bed without watching the rest of the ten o'clock news. "Sounds like the center of the storm is right overhead. The lights have already blinked a couple of times. Might as well call it a day before the power goes off."

She reached for the flashlight in the end table drawer. They had been married long enough for him to know that she was actually upset by the national news reporter's rather biased account that they had just watched of Jack Hatfield's murder and the local sheriff's ability, or lack thereof, to solve such a serious case. He fully intended to solve it; it might take him the rest of his life, but he'd get the killer.

Dalton rolled himself into the large, four-poster bed. Usually he dropped off quickly, sometimes before his wife could even get her makeup removed and a nightgown on. Tonight was an exception; Ginger was already curled on her side, apparently dead to the world. He tried to sleep, but various thoughts flashed off and on in his mind as he lay and listened to the rain beat harder and harder against the bedroom windows.

The heart of the storm was still overhead, complete with thunder boomers that vibrated the house and lightning that lit up the room every few seconds. The wind whistled through the large white pine tree outside their window.

The shadows of the branches waving back and forth on the ceiling reminded him briefly of the days when his children were small and a cardinal would come every spring to make her nest there. Debby and Dan had loved to watch the baby birds start life through the sheer curtains that gave the mamma bird a false sense of privacy.

Dalton rolled over on his side. With Dan away at college in Springfield and Deb married and living in her own home, things were certainly much quieter. No teenagers with bad attitudes, loud music, and bedrooms that looked like toxic waste dumps. No walking the floor until everyone made curfew. Who'd have thought he'd miss that so much?

He never should have let Deb get married while she was still in high school, baby or no baby. At least she'd kept her promise to graduate. Probably shouldn't have let Dan go so far away to college either. He could have just as easily gone to Shawnee and lived at home this year.

Maybe if Deb's baby girl had lived, things would've been different. He still mourned for her. But, probably before they knew it, he and Ginger would likely be grandparents again, even as young as they were. Most of the grandparents he knew were well over fifty. He was still in his early forties.

He hoped that Debby and Chuck had the good sense to wait before trying to start a family again, but he doubted it. He didn't want his little girl to risk suffering another loss anytime soon.

Dalton's mind moved to Mark and Peggy's loss. He wanted to solve this case badly for them, for himself, but most of all for Jack. He felt very uneasy knowing his friend's killer was free while Jack's body lay at the funeral home just a few blocks away.

Miss Mamie's statement to Peters and Edwards that she'd seen Mark Hatfield backed up his alibi that he hadn't left home last night.

He sighed heavily and turned over again. Peggy said she'd had a headache and couldn't go out. He remembered that Jack had mentioned she often had severe migraines.

His thoughts turned to Ruby Miller. Even though she didn't appear to have an alibi, he was having trouble imagining a woman carrying his friend's body up the ladder and maneuvering it onto the arm of the statue. But the fact that she and Jack hadn't been as close lately was something he couldn't ignore. Who could have helped her move a dead body?

And what about the tool salesman they hadn't managed to locate yet? Could he be the key to this case? Dalton pushed the quilt off his legs for the third time, and then pulled it back up.

He wondered how the killer had gotten the body to the statue if he'd murdered Jack elsewhere. And why had Jack worn his costume when it wasn't Halloween or time for the festival? What, if anything, did the costume have to do with his murder?

Ginger rolled over. "What's the matter? Can't you sleep?"

"Sorry, Hon. I thought you'd already dozed off. I'll try to lay still."

"I can't sleep either." Ginger snuggled up against his side and tickled his chest with her fingers. "I think I need something interesting to take my mind off my troubles."

He put his arm out and pulled her closer. "Always happy to oblige."

CHAPTER 11

Late the next morning Dalton left his office and headed to the courthouse to talk to the state's attorney about the recent murder case. He started up the courthouse sidewalk, head down and deep in thought, without looking at the Superman statue until the sound of happy voices penetrated his gloom and caused him to turn and look. The sight of the group gathered there stopped him in his tracks.

It was a wedding party, taking pictures in front of Superman. The bride, sporting a short, off-white dress with a serious tear at the hem turned her tanned, weather-beaten face in Dalton's direction and waved.

"Mornin', Sheriff."

Her smile was full of the joy of the day, even as the wind blew part of her high-piled hairdo dangerously to one side. She wore a man's jacket over her shoulders to ward off the brisk breeze that was moving the clouds out of the area, carrying the heavy rainfall of the previous night with them.

The groom removed the Red Man Chew ball cap that squatted above his wrinkled brow and waved it at Dalton, spitting accurately at the sidewalk below, narrowly missing his own cowboy boots.

"Want to kiss the bride?"

Well, what do you know? Jess and Millie had finally tied the knot.

"It's about time you put a ring on Millie's finger, Jess. Leave a good woman like her running around single, someone's liable to steal her," Dalton shouted back.

The rest of the rather casually dressed friends and relatives swarmed the bride and groom for a group picture. It occurred to Dalton that if that slightly biased national news reporter covering Jack's murder caught a glimpse of this group, she'd quickly pigeonhole the entire wedding party as rednecks. Maybe so, but he'd lived in redneck country all his life, and knew there was more to it than what the stereotype portrayed.

Jess and Millie were the kind of folks who worked hard for a living—physical work, not just mental—and they'd likely live to old age because of it. They were the kind of people who would stop on the side of the road to help a stranger, and the stranger wouldn't have to be afraid to accept that help. Metropolis was still a good place to live, raise a family, and grow old in, despite yesterday's horrific event.

Dalton watched as the bride and groom kissed during a shot. The groom actually removed his hat. He hoped they would have as many happy years of marriage as he'd had. He reluctantly turned and went in the door of the courthouse and up the stairs.

His slightly lighter mood lasted clear to the door of the state's attorney's office. He generally had a good relationship with her, but this case worried him. No leads yet and no real suspects to report. The phones at the detention center had rung all morning. Folks all over the area were demanding quick answers, and he didn't have any. He took a deep breath and went in.

Terri Reynolds, the only female state's attorney in the history of Massac County, was not in her usual good humor. Dalton remembered that she'd had a huge crush on Jack Hatfield. He and Ginger had even double-dated with Hatfield and the former cheerleader a time or two. He could tell from the frown on her face that he was in for it.

"The phones have been ringing all morning. My secretary hasn't even had time for a bathroom break. Neither have I for that matter," she snapped. "Between the media demanding information and Jack's old high school teammates demanding the death penalty—assuming we do catch his killer—I can't get any work done. I sincerely hope you have news for me."

"The coroner has given us a preliminary report. Jack was strangled and then decapitated. It was likely someone he knew, or he wouldn't have turned his back to him. No motive as far as we can see, yet."

"No arrests either, I take it? Did you see the news last night? That reporter made us all look like a bunch of country bumpkins that couldn't win a game of Clue."

Dalton swallowed hard, opened his mouth to speak, and was cut off by a volley of questions fired at him with the precision and accuracy of an Uzi.

"How could anyone have hung a body on that statue, even at night, without being seen? Did the lab find any prints? And can we match them to anyone?" Her eyes bored into his like laser beams. "Do you have any suspects yet? Any clues at all?"

"The killer used the janitor's ladder. We sent it to Carbondale for testing. I doubt we'll find any prints. Big Ed Simmons might have seen something, but he's a total blank."

Before he could answer any more of her questions, as politely and vaguely as possible, his radio crackled and he reached for the volume control, feeling like a death row prisoner who had just received the long-hoped-for call from the governor. Means wouldn't be trying to reach the sheriff during this meeting if it weren't urgent.

"Sheriff, you hear me?" Means blasted out. Means recent habit of shouting into either the radio or the telephone made Dalton wonder if the dispatcher was beginning to have hearing problems.

"Yes, George, half the county can hear you. What is it?"

"A nine-one-one call just came in from Dr. Tracey's cell phone. She's out to the Windhorst farm. Says you better come right on out there. Claims her and Sam found a dead body buried there, though what a veterinarian is doing digging around in the ground is more than I can—"

Dalton cut Means off in mid-speculation. "George, did she say whose body they found?"

"Nope, just said to get you out there right away. Sounded out of breath, like she'd been running. Then she hung up. Kinda rude if you ask me."

"Tell the deputies to meet me in front of the office. Call her back and let her know that we'll be there shortly." Dalton swung around and headed out the door.

"Terrific," the state's attorney bellowed after him. "Just what we need. Another body. Joe, I want answers, and I want them yesterday. Do you understand?"

"I'll do my best, just like I always do," he yelled over his shoulder. "I'll get back to you as soon as possible." Meaning whenever he absolutely couldn't put it off any longer.

CHAPTER 12

Dalton swung into driveway of the Windhorst farm several minutes later, slinging gravel across the long twists and turns up the hill toward the old house. He hung a sharp left at the house then went downhill a ways to the large old barn. Dalton's deputies were close behind in two other county vehicles. He turned off the flashing lights and heaved himself out of the driver's seat. Car doors slammed behind him as the deputies followed suit.

Sam Windhorst, elbows and knees protruding through the holes in his coverall, nervously paced back and forth in front of the barn door, his boots making a rut in the dirt. His faithful shepherd mix, Gypsy, followed every footstep, watching her master's face for reassurance.

Dr. Tracey Coltharp was propped against the fence that adjoined the barn, elbows on the top rail. She appeared to be sucking in fresh air and concentrating on the panoramic view provided by the Windhorst farm. Also dressed in a worn coverall and large rubber boots, she looked more like a Hee Haw regular than the pretty young veterinarian she was.

"George said you found a body behind the barn, no details. Do you know who it is?" Dalton addressed the question to the young veterinarian, since she'd placed the call, but Windhorst burst in with the answer.

"Worst thing I ever seen," he said angrily, gesturing toward the side of the barn. "It's a little bitty baby, maybe even a newborn. Looks like the mamma just up and had it and dumped it there behind my barn. Gypsy found it."

Dalton was slightly relieved. All the way out on the drive to the farm, he'd been speculating this body was the second in a series by Jack Hatfield's killer.

"We both thought Gypsy was just reacting to the birth of the calves, but afterward, she kept running toward the back of the barn, barking frantically," Dr. Tracey said. "We followed her and the smell led us the rest of the way to the body. It's pretty rough back there."

"Okay, let's have a look."

Dalton fell into step with the weathered farmer, Colthorp slogging along beside them, while the deputies brought up the rear. Gypsy bounced and barked alongside Windhorst.

"Yes, girl, we know you found it." Windhorst reached down in mid-stride and patted Gypsy's head.

"Awful business," Windhorst said. "Cain't imagine anyone 'round here doing something like this."

Windhorst led the group to a stand of large bushes at the fencerow behind the barn. He pointed to a depression in the ground where the recent heavy rain had washed open what appeared to be a hastily dug, then refilled, hole.

A large plastic trash bag spilled out of the hole like a fountain of black oil. The foul smell weaved itself among the other barn smells, overpowering them with its fetid stench.

Dalton stopped dead in his tracks when he saw a tiny foot sticking up as if it had attempted to kick it's way out of the shallow grave. He heard a couple of sharp intakes of breath behind him.

Dalton turned to his deputies. "Secure this area for the crime lab team. Peters, you take Dr. Tracey's statement, I'll take Mr. Windhorst's. Edwards and Wilson photograph and measure the area. I see the coroner coming up the drive. Doody, wave him back here, then look around for evidence."

Dalton turned back to the farmer. "Other than the hunters who have access to your fields, have you seen anyone around who didn't have permission the past few days?

Windhorst wiped his forehead with his kerchief and stuffed it back into one of the dozen or so pockets in his coverall.

"The barn purty well blocks our view of that part of the fencerow an' the bush where the body is. Tisn't likely we'da seen anyone there. Never noticed anything unusual 'til today. Sure hope you catch whoever left that little 'un there. Wouldn't mind a few minutes alone in the barn with 'em, m'self."

The tone in Windhorst's voice made Dalton look up from his note pad into the crinkled, brown face. Windhorst might be only two years shy of being able to draw his Social Security, but he was still as rawboned and wiry as Dalton remembered when he was Dalton's scoutmaster.

Most likely that came from having done a man's work every day of his life since early boyhood. Dalton knew that the perpetrator of this crime would be much safer spending life in jail than spending five minutes alone with Windhorst in his barn.

"Yer welcome to look around all you need, use any of my stuff if you have to," Windhorst offered. "I gotta get back to work."

"Thanks, Mr. Windhorst. I appreciate it. I'll let you know when I find out anything."

"Sorry about young Hatfield. Hope you catch ever who killed him, too. What's happening to Massac County?"

Having said his piece, Sam Windhorst placed his cap firmly back on his head and whistled for Gypsy. They both climbed into the cab of a large tractor parked beside the barn. Windhorst fired up the noisy old engine, and they made their escape to a nearby field.

Dalton turned to the young veterinarian. "After you finish

with Deputy Peters, you're free to leave. I'm sure you're anxious to get back to work as well. We'll call you if we need anything else."

"Thanks, Sheriff. I do need to get back to town. Mavis Thompson's Shih Tzu is about to give birth and she expects me to hold Mademoiselle's paw all through the procedure."

Dalton rolled his eyes. Thompson made a fortune off those puppies and guarded them like Fort Knox. His office was notified every time a stray male dog crossed her back yard.

"Ginger told me that you've been volunteering to help get the new humane society under way. We certainly need a shelter in this county."

"Yeah. I spent most of yesterday doing a spay/neuter clinic with them. Would you believe some people actually sneaked their pets across the county line to get the freebie? Next time I'll demand birth certificates from both pet and owner."

Dalton grinned at the young vet.

"Good luck with the shelter, Tracey. If your group can get the stray dogs off the street, that'll get Mavis off our backs, and we can get on with the business of solving crime."

"My pleasure. Mavis's business pays the light bill, but I'd much rather be out in the county, helping farmers like Sam. His best breeder was in real trouble this morning. Luckily we got the calves out safely, and she's busy doing her mamma thing."

Coltharp glanced at the shallow grave, winced, and turned to Deputy Peters.

Jeffords joined Dalton near the grave. The coroner couldn't move the body until the crime lab team excavated it from the shallow burial site, and they had yet to arrive.

"I opened the garbage bag a little to get a closer look. The baby was a newborn. The cord's still attached. There's a large pool of congealed blood around his body, so my guess is he bled to death. The autopsy will show if there were any other

75

contributing factors."

The coroner turned back to the body. "He looks fully developed, even has a small patch of wavy blond hair, so he probably wasn't premature. Oh, and one other thing; I can see most of the afterbirth on the far side of the body. It looks like a sizable piece of it is missing."

"Meaning?" Dalton asked.

"Meaning it could have been lost between the birth and burying the baby here. But if it didn't all come out, there is a very sick mother somewhere."

"If the afterbirth is still attached, that means this baby wasn't born in a hospital, right?" Dalton asked. "And that means no footprints, no records, no way to identify him. Terrific."

"He was probably born in a motel room or somebody's bedroom, although, I suppose a car is a possibility, too. With any luck, the mother will seek medical help for her condition, and you still might be able to find her. If she doesn't, the chances are pretty good that it'll kill her."

At least the part about the missing afterbirth gave them a hope of finding the parents. This was, after all, Metropolis and not Chicago or some other large city. The sheriff's office didn't usually have to handle two murders in such a short time; they rarely got two murders in one month. If the mother experienced serious problems, that might give his office a chance to locate her. And there was always the forensic pathologist. He might come up with something. Dalton joined the deputies in their search for evidence.

***

By lunchtime Dalton was able to leave the scene and drive over to Smallman's Restaurant on Highway 45. His stomach had returned to its usual cast iron state, and he was hungry for one of their home-style meals and a piece of mile-high meringue pie. The deputies were wrapping up their part of the morning's work and would follow within minutes.

The atmosphere and decor at Smallman's had not changed in several decades, which suited Dalton and the other regulars just fine. The vinyl seats were cracked, but comfortable. He noted the large variety of crème pies that appeared to be suspended upside down in the mirrored glass case.

As usual, nearly every seat in the place was full, with conversations taking place around tables and across the room. The jukebox blasted out a soulful country tune about lost love.

It took Dalton a couple of minutes to work his way to a table in the back corner, his progress hampered by questions. Everyone wanted to know the identity of the body found at Windhorst's farm. Scanners. Dalton would love to outlaw them. And they wanted to know how the investigation into Jack Hatfield's death was proceeding. He answered as politely and vaguely as possible, before he finally hitched up his pants, and took a seat.

The waitress arrived and plopped Dalton's water, coffee, and a large, warm piece of coconut pie on the wobbly table in front of him.

"Thanks."

She nodded, and with all the speed and grace of an aging turtle, headed back toward the kitchen to place his lunch order without bothering to ask what he wanted. It probably would have thrown her entire day off if he'd ordered a different meal from his usual liver and onions, smothered in brown gravy, with mashed potatoes, spiced apples, slaw, and corn bread on the side. He'd never been willing to risk it.

Dalton's deputies entered the restaurant, joined their boss at his table in the back, and received the same treatment from the waitress.

While they waited for the food to arrive, they discussed in

low tones the most recent crime and how Dalton wanted them to proceed with the investigation. Noisy conversations at the other tables about the price of crops and the recent welcome rain, punctuated by loud laughter, provided a cover for them to talk without being overheard.

"It seems likely that the baby's mother was some local teenager who hid her pregnancy and then disposed of him either alone or with the help of the father or a friend." Dalton swallowed a bite of pie.

He repeated Jeffords's preliminary report to them, particularly the possibility that the mother might need medical attention if the afterbirth hadn't completely separated from her womb.

"Doody, check out Massac County hospital and all the doctor's offices."

Doody gave a curt nod.

"Wilson, you take the high school and college. Get the names of any pregnant students."

"Okay."

"Peters and Edwards, you check Paducah. Split it between you, one of you taking the schools and half the doctor's offices. The other can take both of the hospitals and the rest of the doctors on your list." He paused for the last bite of pie. "It's possible that someone came from across the river to bury the baby here."

Dalton glanced around the table. Billy Wilson leaned over to compare notes with Craig Edwards on measurements taken at the scene.

Doody Jenson sat with arms folded on the table, head down, lost in thought. Dalton noticed that Jenson hadn't even bothered teasing the waitress in his usual manner. He'd heard scuttlebutt around the department that the Jensons were trying to conceive without much luck. If that were true, then this case would likely sink Jenson's usual good humor.

78

Peters stared out the window between sips of iced tea, apparently deep in thought. Dalton had rarely seen this particular deputy's feathers ruffled. Maybe there was a chink in her seemingly thick armor after all?

The waitress arrived with their meals balanced everywhere but on her head, plopped the dishes down in front of them, and asked if anyone needed anything else. No one did. She readjusted the seldom-used pencil behind her ear and began her slow-motion trip back to the kitchen.

Instructions having been given and received by all present, Dalton watched as the deputies dug in.

CHAPTER 13

The afternoon had been long and fruitless, but Doody Jensen was too angry to feel tired. His jaws ached from the effort of smiling and looking normal while he interviewed people at Massac Memorial Hospital and the various doctor's offices in Metropolis. He could have easily chewed several ten-penny nails in two if he'd had any handy. He was glad he didn't.

Rather than go straight home after his shift ended and take his anger home to his wife, Doody had driven to Massac Park. He'd passed several walkers and joggers on the meandering asphalt drive. He pulled his car to the edge of the grass near a play area that overlooked the river and turned off the engine.

Tucked into a corner at the south edge of Metropolis, Fort Massac Park ran east along the Ohio River under the I-24 Bridge, and ended near Highway 145. Doody glanced over at the replica of the original fort that drew hundreds of visitors every year, as did its museum. He'd loved playing soldier there as a child.

The front that had brought the recent heavy rainstorm through southern Illinois had dragged a short spell of warm weather along behind it, enticing residents back outside for the afternoon.

On his right, a family picnicked, and on his left, a father pushed the swings for his two youngsters as they squealed with delight.

Doody often ate his lunch here, so he could watch the towboats push the heavy barges up and down the river and listen to their mournful horns signaling each other. He usually enjoyed seeing the children at play, but not today.

How could anyone put a beautiful, healthy newborn in a plastic bag, let it bleed to death, and bury it like last week's garbage? Especially when people like Michelle and himself were praying for a child of their own.

People didn't get upset over out-of-wedlock pregnancies like they did fifty years ago. And even if they did, letting the baby die wasn't necessary. There were safe places to leave unwanted newborns. The baby could be alive and well in a good home.

Doody wondered briefly if the parents had been too young and dumb to know about tying off the cord, but quickly dismissed the idea. Kids saw enough on TV nowadays to nearly be able to do brain surgery. He couldn't imagine someone not knowing enough to tie off the cord, particularly after the baby began to lose blood through it. Nope, this must have been deliberate. He ground his teeth. He would love a few minutes alone with whoever had done this.

Maybe if he and Michelle had been able to have kids this wouldn't have hit him quite so hard. The fact that it was his fault that they didn't have any children only made matters worse. He wanted to give Michelle the world, but she didn't want the whole world, she just wanted his kids. And so did he. What if those expensive treatments didn't work? What if they couldn't adopt? Would he be enough for her? Or would she let the disappointment become a wall between them?

He wanted to yell or hit something—or worse—someone. Particularly that someone who had buried the unidentified infant at the Windhorst farm. He pounded his fist on the steering wheel in an effort to vent his frustrations, but that didn't work. He balled his fists and rubbed his eyelids. He told himself it was to wipe away the sweat. After all, grown men didn't cry, did they? Especially grown men who were trained sheriff's deputies?

Doody heaved a deep sigh and turned his thoughts back to the investigation. This murder was going to be on all the local newscasts and in the papers. In fact, with any luck, the national news media would probably pounce on the story as well. They were still keeping an eye on the Metropolis area hoping for news of an arrest in the Hatfield case. He'd fielded a couple of their calls. The death of this infant would give them something else to focus on while they waited. The more publicity this case got, the better the chances of solving it.

Folks in this area were conservative, holding tight to their family values. Any person who allowed an unwanted child to die did not fit into those values. People might remember who had suddenly lost weight or who had been ill at the right time, and they might pass that information along. Rumors would circulate like wildfire, and one or two might turn into leads, if they were real lucky.

Most parents who caused the deaths of their children got caught these days. This pair wouldn't get away with it if the mother sought medical treatment. Or if Deputy Doody Jenson had anything to say about it.

His anger now channeled into finding out who had dumped the baby boy into the shallow grave, Doody at last felt able to go home, face Michelle, and answer her questions about how the case was going. He cranked the engine and eased his car out of the parking area and back onto the asphalt road.

Instead of heading to the main park entrance, Doody turned onto the small gravel road that wandered off through the wooded game reserve adjacent to the park. The woods there were cool and quiet. The longer drive would give him a few minutes more before he had to face Michelle. He knew she would be as upset as he was.

He drove slowly through the dusk, hoping to see a deer in this wild section of the park. He enjoyed seeing their heads bob up and down as they watched the humans watching them. So far the deer seemed to be elsewhere.

He was nearing the end of the road when he saw a truck parked in a hiking trail entrance. It looked like the truck Billy Wilson drove.

Doody tapped the breaks and peered at the license plate on the back of the truck. It was Billy's. The plate read Wilson 55, his name and jersey number from high school. Maybe his fellow deputy had come to the woods to unwind as well. Doody was reaching for the horn when he realized Billy wasn't alone in the truck. A woman sat beside him.

Well, "sat" wasn't exactly the right word. They were both leaning heavily against the passenger door. From what Doody was able to observe, Billy was either practicing mouth-to-mouth resuscitation on the woman or kissing her in a way that would have made most high school boys envious. Doody could see just enough of the woman to realize that she was a brunette. That certainly wasn't Billy's blonde wife. Intent on each other, the couple had neither seen nor heard Doody's approach. He decided to creep by and not interrupt them. It wasn't right for a man to fool around on his wife. Doody would have plenty to say to Billy later.

As his car inched by, Doody wondered who the woman was. He didn't wonder long. Her small red Volkswagen was backed in beside Billy's truck. The license plate read Ruby 1. Ruby Miller, former girlfriend of Jack Hatfield and current suspect in his murder. And yet there was Billy parked in the woods playing lip-lock with her. What was going on? The anger flared again inside Doody like fire through an open furnace door.

He drove to a sharp curve where the park ended and the

gravel woodland drive merged into the county road, and backed onto the right shoulder near a fence. It had gotten darker by the time he reached the fence, so Billy wouldn't be able to spot him until he was ready to be seen.

He'd bet Ruby would drive back through the park to the front entrance since it was closer to her home. Billy would have to come out the back, quite a distance from the front, to avoid arousing suspicion. He would catch Billy there and give him a piece of his mind. Here, at last, was someone he could rightly vent his anger on. Doody settled in and ruminated on how best to blast Billy out of the water.

He rolled the driver's side window down to catch the breeze that rattled the few remaining leaves on nearby trees. He listened as the tree frogs sang and smelled the smoke that blew toward him from a house down the road where an elderly man burned a leaf pile in the ditch in front of his house.

When he heard Billy's truck coming toward him in the dusk, Doody fired up his engine again and eased out onto the road. He stopped in the middle of the curve, effectively cutting off the truck's path. Apparently recognizing his co-worker in the driver's seat, Billy stopped, rolled down his window, and said, "Hey, Doody, what's going on?"

"That's just what I'd like to know, Billy. Pull over. We need to talk."

(HAPTER 14

Doody backed his car onto the right shoulder of the road again, and Billy turned and parked in front of him. He wasn't smiling as he slid into the front seat of Doody's car and folded his long legs under the dash. There was an uncomfortable pause as each waited for the other to speak. Finally, Doody broke the silence.

"What's going on between you and Ruby Miller? I saw the two of you back there." Doody tipped his head toward the woods.

"We were just talking. Ruby's upset about Hatfield's death. I was trying to comfort her."

Doody snorted. "If that's your idea of comforting, I'd be very interested to know what you'd call fooling around."

"Okay, so we kissed. No big deal. I was hugging her and it just sorta happened. I won't let it happen again. Happy now?"

"It's more than that, and you and I both know it. Ruby is a suspect in the murder of her boyfriend. Your job is to investigate her, not hide in the woods and make out with her."

It was time to get tough. "You're sleeping with her, aren't you?"

When Billy didn't answer, Doody's anger exploded.

"How could you do this? How could you cheat on Barb? You're married to one of the nicest women in Metropolis, in all of Massac County for that matter, not to mention clean, decent, . . . and she's the mother of your children."

He ran out of arguments and breath at the same time.

Billy stared out the window, his jaw working, obviously trying to contain his own anger. Doody knew his words had hit home.

"You don't want to talk to me about this? Fine. We'll see what Dalton has to say about you meeting secretly in the woods with a murder suspect."

Billy hit the door with his fist. "It's always so easy for you, isn't it, Doody? Everything is black and white, no in-between."

A silence followed stretching out so long that Doody was about to reach for the keys, chuck Billy out of the car, and leave. He was surprised when Billy finally spoke.

"We've been seeing each other for about a month."

"She's Hatfield's girlfriend, or she was. Everyone in town knows that. And you're married. How could you let this happen?"

"It caught me by surprise. I was working some overtime, and I answered a nine-one-one call at Ruby's house. She thought she heard someone outside. Hatfield was busy with some business thing and couldn't come over. She was terrified and with good reason." Wilson let out a breath of air with a whoosh.

"Someone had loosened the screws on the screen covering her bedroom window. I found some tracks in the mud near her driveway, but the guy was long gone. We haven't caught him yet. When I left, she was shaking like a leaf."

There was another long pause as he struggled for the words to explain.

"I hadn't seen Ruby in a long time. She's still as pretty as she was in high school. She had a crush on me back then, but I couldn't see anyone but Barb."

He paused again and looked down at his hands, as if he could find the answer to his troubles there.

"Like I said, I felt sorry for Ruby, alone in that house and so scared, so I stopped by on my way home to check on her. She gave me a hug to thank me. Next thing I knew, we were kissing like two love-starved teenagers. I tried to leave, honest, Doody, but I couldn't."

Doody's jaws were beginning to ache again from clenching them.

"You beat all I ever saw. Just that simple, huh? Didn't think about your wife, didn't think about your kids, how this might hurt them. How could you even look at another woman much less fall into bed with her?"

The pause was so long this time that Doody was certain Billy wasn't going to answer. As he drew breath to shout again, Billy spoke so quietly Doody could barely hear him.

"It isn't always that simple, Doody. Nothing ever is. You asked how I could look at another woman. Suppose I told you that all I'm allowed to do at home is look but I can't touch?"

Doody looked at Billy. "What's that supposed to mean?"

"What it means in plain English, Doody, is that Barb and I rarely have sex." His voice was like lead. He unwrapped himself and turned in the seat to face Doody.

"I need you to keep this to yourself, Doody. Hopefully you'll understand. It isn't something I'm proud of, not something I'd willingly tell. I haven't even told this to Ruby."

Doody squirmed in his seat.

"Barb thinks sex is dirty and that men are dirty for wanting it. She cringes every time I come near her. Can you imagine what it's like to lay in bed beside the woman you love and not be able to touch her? Her attitude has just about killed any feelings I ever had for her."

Doody was speechless. He couldn't imagine living like that, not being able to touch Michelle.

"When Barb and I were dating she wasn't very keen on

sex. I figured maybe she was just scared because we weren't married. I figured she'd loosen up after we had some place to be alone besides the back seat of my car. She didn't. She got worse."

He took a deep breath and continued. "At first she just insisted that all the lights be out, so I couldn't see her. Then she started putting me off more. After Patty was born, Barb pretty much cut me off all together."

Doody tried to picture Barb as an iceberg and failed. She always seemed so happy, so enthusiastic whenever he and Michelle ran into her at the grocery.

"On the rare, and I do mean rare, occasions she does give in, she just lays there through the whole thing like a tree limb. No, actually I think a tree limb would be more giving. Are you starting to get the picture, Doody?"

The edge in Billy's words made Doody cringe. Hurt and anger had replaced calm self-confidence. Doody was silent for a moment. His own little honey had always been so loving, so giving. What he was hearing was way over his head.

"Can't you get some help, counseling or something, for both of you?" Doody finally asked.

"She won't go for counseling. And I can't leave her either. At least not yet. Barb wants a home and family, and she's determined to keep them, no matter what the cost to either of us."

"I don't understand." Doody said.

"Barb says if I leave her, or even mention our home life to anyone, she'll divorce me and take the kids. She says she'll turn them against me by telling them that I abused her. It isn't true. I'd never do a thing like that."

Doody nodded. He didn't believe Billy would ever hit a woman, and Barb didn't strike him as the type who'd have stood still for it. She'd probably have hit Billy back and then packed up and left.

"I could take just about anything except losing my kids, Doody. That's the only reason I've stuck it out for this long."

Doody took a deep breath and tried to make sense of what he'd heard.

"What are you going to do about Ruby? This isn't fair to her, and if Barb finds out, you probably will lose your kids. Have you tried to break it off?" Doody figured he wasn't going to like the answer.

"Of course I have." Billy gestured angrily. "I've tried several times, and so has Ruby."

More quietly he said, "She doesn't want me to lose my family any more than I do, and she didn't want to hurt Hatfield."

Wait a minute. Possible motive? "But that gives Ruby a reason for killing Hatfield, her affair with you. Maybe she wanted to get rid of him to be with you. Did you think of that?"

This time it was Billy who snorted. "No, Doody, I didn't. I know she didn't kill Jack Hatfield because I was with her that whole evening. And before you ask, no, I didn't kill him either."

Doody had the grace to blush at that. He was glad it was too dark by now for Billy to see.

"Barb and the girls were going out of town with her folks for a couple of days," Billy continued. "I figured I'd be alone, but Ruby called me that morning and said Hatfield had cancelled their dinner date. She wanted to take me out, some place special. I was mad at Barb and I wanted to be with Ruby. I decided to risk it. Guess it's a good thing I did."

Doody shook his head in amazement.

"She took me to some little restaurant over in Kentucky, in the Land Between the Lakes area. It's an out-of-the-way place. Not many Illinois people go there, so we figured we'd be safe."

"Well, that's a relief. For a minute there I was afraid I was going to have to investigate you," Doody said. "Can anyone verify that you two were there?"

"Yeah. While we were eating, the guy at the next table got into it with his wife. He drew back and I was afraid he'd hit her, so I stood up, flashed my badge, and told him to cool off."

"Weren't you afraid that'd blow your cover?"

"Didn't really stop to think about it then. Just reacted. Anyhow, they paid up and left. That was around nine-thirty or so, the time the autopsy report says Hatfield was hung on the statue. The manager can verify that we were there at that time. He paid for our dessert as a 'thank you', so he'll remember."

"When Dalton finds out that you're sleeping with a suspect, even one with an alibi, he's still going to have your hide."

Billy looked sideways at Doody.

"Okay, okay, I won't say anything to Dalton right now, unless I have to. But you need to tell him. It's going to come out eventually. You see that, don't you? If I caught on, somebody else will. Better it comes from you."

"I keep hoping we'll catch the murderer. Then none of this would have to come out. Dalton would never have to know."

"You turned in a false report about Ruby to him. He needs to know that she has an alibi, so he can count her out as a suspect. It just isn't right for you to let Dalton think she might be somehow involved in Hatfield's murder."

"Come on, Doody, help me out here. Give me a chance to work something out. Maybe no one else but you will ever have to know. You owe me."

Billy waited for an answer. Doody squirmed again. Billy had saved his hide more than once. He did owe Billy, big time.

Doody's troublesome conscience told him he ought to drive straight to the sheriff's house and tell him everything. But his big heart told him he should help a friend.

After a brief struggle, heart won. Since neither Ruby nor Billy was actually involved in the murder, why get them both into trouble? Doody had been at the wrong end of Dalton's anger more than once. He wasn't eager to shove anyone else into the firestorm.

"Okay, I won't tell Dalton what I know unless it becomes absolutely necessary to the case." Doody reached for the keys in the ignition.

"If that happens, I'll tell him myself. I won't get you involved at all. I'll take my licks when the time comes."

Wilson pulled his long legs out from under the dash and got out of the car. He leaned back into the window and said, "Thanks, Doody. I know how you feel about this, and I really appreciate your help."

Doody sighed. He knew the promise was going to cause him some sleepless nights. He started the car and headed home, thankful for Michelle every mile of the way.

CHAPTER 15

"Tough day, huh?" Ginger sounded as tired as he felt. He wondered briefly what she'd been doing to make her look so worn out.

"Lately, they all seem to be tough," he replied as he released her from their nightly hug.

"I went to Jack's wake and signed the book for both of us. I figured you wouldn't be able to make it."

"Thanks. I meant to stop by the funeral home, but I ran out of time. Wonder why they only held it from four to six? That didn't give the locals much time to get by there," Dalton said.

"According to Mark, Peggy's migraine hasn't gone away since Jack died. He wanted to make it as easy on her as possible. If you ask me, they both look awful."

He plopped his large frame down into his usual kitchen chair and sniffed the air as she ladled out two bowls of navy bean soup loaded with chunks of potatoes, onions, and ham bits, another of his favorites.

"I heard at the Planet about a baby being buried in a pasture somewhere near the highway. Marty Hoggs is still off chasing geese somewhere in Canada, so I got the job of writing a feature story about abandoned infants. Most of them don't survive."

She plunked a bowl down in front of him. Now he knew

what was wrong. She'd heard about the latest murder. He'd been so busy, he'd forgotten about her new job at the paper.

"You'd think people would learn that dumping a child isn't the end of their problems. It's just the beginning. They said your office was investigating. Figured you'd need a warm dinner after that. I hope you catch the parents and put them *under* the jail."

"I'm sure going to try to do that, catch them, I mean. Sam Windhorst wants a few minutes alone in his barn with the baby's killer. Doody looks like a bomb hunting for a place to explode. The state's attorney wants my hide on her wall, and Buck and some of the city council are willing to help her get it."

He shook his head and reached for a corn muffin. No matter how bad things got, it never seemed to affect his appetite for very long. Sometimes he wished it would.

"What about you? For someone who's always wanted to graduate from the gardening page to the front page, you don't seem to be very happy with your new assignments."

"Actually, I'm thoroughly enjoying the new job. Much as I love gardening, there's only so much you can say about pine bark mulch verses riverbed rocks in one column."

She passed him the butter. "Problem is, when Marty decides to return to civilization and wants his job back, Ken will have to give it to him. They're married to sisters. Ken can only carry this 'teach Marty a lesson' business so far."

"What will you do then? Go back to your old column?"

"I don't know. Maybe. I've been toying with the idea of writing a book. I just don't know if I'm ready for a project that big."

Ginger broke a corn muffin in half. "Tell me more about your day."

"We have no evidence as to who the parents were. If we're real lucky, someone will call in with a tip about a woman who was pregnant, isn't any more, and has no baby to show for it. We're putting the word out in the media, and the deputies checked all the area hospitals and doctors, just in case. Now we wait for a break."

"Anything new on Jack's murder?"

"No. We still haven't been able to contact the salesman Jack met with the night he died. I'm hoping he'll be able to tell us something. Beyond that, we just keep hitting dead ends."

"You'll find the answers. You always do."

He wished he had as much faith in his skills as she did.

Dalton finished his second helping and relinquished his bowl. His wife stored the leftovers and reminded him to secure the lid on the large outdoor trashcan.

"You'd think we lived in the woods instead of the middle of town," he protested.

"Tell that to the raccoons. They scattered the Killion's trash all over their back yard last night. Gene swears he had moth crystals taped to the lid, but it didn't help. And fences are certainly useless at keeping those rascals out."

Dalton came back inside, shot the bolt on the kitchen door, and sauntered toward the living room couch to hunt for the remote control. Before he could use it, Ginger reached out and took his hand.

"We need to talk," she told him.

"Okay."

Why did wives always want to talk when their husbands were physically and mentally exhausted? It was hard enough to express himself plainly to her when he was well rested.

"Joe, I…" she lost her composure and started to cry.

He put his arms around her, suddenly really worried about what was going on.

"Honey, what is it? Is something wrong with you or one of the kids? Talk to me."

Ginger wiped her eyes with the back of her hand. "I had

my annual checkup and mammogram last week. They called me with the results today."

"And?" he prompted.

"There's a new lump, or mass, or something. They aren't sure how serious it is. Dr. Lewis thinks I should see a surgeon." She reached across him for the box of tissues on the end table.

"He made me an appointment with a doctor in Paducah for tomorrow morning. The surgeon may do a biopsy in his office with a needle. Or he may decide to schedule surgery."

Dalton's chest tightened.

"Joe, I'm so scared. I don't know what to do. Could you possibly take tomorrow morning off and go with me? I asked Debby, but she said she already had an appointment that she just can't break."

He hated doctor's offices, only going when she dragged him in and left him no choice; but no way could he let her face this by herself.

"Of course I will. I'll call the office first thing and tell them I'll be late," he assured her. "I'll get Peters to go to Jack's funeral in case we don't get back from Paducah in time."

She snuggled up against him. "Thanks. Having you there will make it much easier. If we get through in time, we should go to Jack's funeral together."

"Okay, if you're up to it after the doctor's office. What else did Dr. Lewis say?"

He tried to sound calm, but his heart was hammering inside his chest. Didn't cancer run in families? Suddenly, he couldn't remember anything he'd ever heard about it.

"That's all his girl told me. She didn't seem to know anything beyond Dr. Lewis wanting the surgeon to see me." She blew her nose into the tissue.

"I know I'm a prime candidate for breast cancer. Mother and Aunt Jesse both had it. It's always been a worry in the back of my mind, but somehow I really wasn't expecting it to come up right now. I check myself regularly, do all the things I'm supposed to do."

His chest got even tighter. Ginger's mother had died young, before her grandchildren were born. Her Aunt Jessie had been a tough old bird. The whole family had thought nothing could ever beat her until the cancer kept returning, more serious each time.

He held Ginger close and told her everything would be fine. He hoped he was right. All the major problems he'd been dealing with suddenly became minor when faced with the possibility of losing her. He didn't even dare let that thought take root.

He'd won her heart when he'd dissected a frog for her in their high school biology class. He'd quickly gotten used to being number one in her life. They'd married young, had kids young, but had never lost their passion for each other.

They'd never had much private time. That had been a luxury they'd only discovered when the children left home. What if that time was about to run out? What would he do without her? Best not to dwell on that. They'd have the test and deal with the results then. Meanwhile, he'd pray harder than he ever had.

She dried her eyes and sat up straighter, apparently jacking up her courage while he struggled with his. He reached for the remote again, not knowing what else to say to her.

"Let's watch TV upstairs where it's a little more comfortable." She gave him a wicked grin and reached for his hand. The remote slid across the coffee table.

CHAPTER 16

The next morning the surgeon came into the room with a bright cheery smile on his face and met two unsmiling people. He did a thorough breast exam while Dalton struggled not to punch his lights out. He'd never stopped to think about what, exactly, a breast exam entailed. Never realized just how intimately a doctor would have to touch her.

"I'd like to do a biopsy and see what we're dealing with."

The surgeon reached for the longest needle Dalton had ever seen, and a quick wash of sweat bathed his forehead. Ginger squeezed his hand until he winced. The surgeon held up the syringe with dark fluid drawn from the lump. Did the dark color mean anything? He was afraid to ask.

"The lab will send back their report in a few days. We'll call you with the results. Try not to worry until then. Most of these turn out to be nothing serious."

"Thank you, Doctor," Ginger responded. "Is the fluid always that dark?"

"Sometimes. The color doesn't tell us anything one way or the other. If the results of the tests are negative, surgery won't be necessary, at least for now. I will want to see you again in a few months, just to be safe."

The surgeon smiled his way out of the room.

Ginger dressed in a hurry, apparently as eager as he was to be out of the doctor's office. They grabbed an early lunch before heading back to Metropolis for the funeral.

She chatted away about his current cases, the kids, the need to get the house ready for winter, her writing, the funeral they were about to attend—everything under the sun except what the biopsy might show. No use dealing with that issue until the time came. He kept up his end of the conversation as best he could.

They arrived at the funeral home to find the mourners lined up outside waiting to view the body and greet the family. The coroner motioned Dalton and Ginger in through a side door.

Dalton turned to his wife. "Better snag us a couple of seats near the back while you can. I need to speak to Mark and Peggy."

He squeezed her arm and began to push through the crowd standing around, gawking, and whispering to each other. Dalton wondered who was operating all the local businesses since nearly the whole town seemed to be crammed into Jeffords and McCann Funeral Home.

Peggy was sobbing in the arms of Miss Mamie Timsley on the pew reserved for family. Mark stood near the casket shaking hands with those who came up to pay their respects and looking like a fish out of water in a suit that smelled strongly of mothballs. To Dalton's relief, the casket was closed.

"Thanks for coming, Sheriff. Jack would have appreciated it."

"Sorry to be here under these circumstances." Stock comment to a grieving relative. What else could you say?

Dalton wondered what his old friend would think about how he was handling this murder case and the lack of any solid clues or suspects.

"I just want you to know, Mark, we won't give up on this case. I'll find out who did this to Jack, no matter what it takes." Tough promise, but he meant it.

Mark nodded and Dalton went to find his seat.

He took the aisle seat on Ginger's right. Linda Peters edged sideways into the pew and took the seat on Ginger's left.

Dalton heard her whisper to Ginger. "How did your visit to the surgeon go?"

"Okay, I guess. He's really nice. I liked the way he treated me, staying in the room to answer my questions and ease my fears instead of edging toward the door as soon as the exam was over. But the biopsy wasn't much fun."

"I know what you mean. I had one after the baby was born. Just the size of the needle was enough to make me want to run. Pretty painful. When will you know the results?"

"In a few days. His office will call me."

"I'll keep the positive thoughts going for you."

"Thanks."

The organ music grew louder, signaling the beginning of the service. The wall of flowers on Dalton's right pumped out an overwhelming fragrance as the minister droned on. With so many people now stuffed into each pew or scrunched in folding chairs on the aisle, the room had become warm and muggy.

Dalton's eyes roamed over the heads in front of him. Ruby Miller sat in the second pew from the front, looking like she'd been carved from stone. She'd always seemed placid enough when Dalton encountered her at his dentist's office. Hard to picture her as a cold-blooded killer, but who knew how she might have reacted if Jack had called off their long-running relationship? The problem was if she did it, how did she get his body on the statue?

Mark and Peggy were hunched together on the front row with Miss Mamie. Could either of them have killed the brother they were so dependent on?

What about that elusive tool salesman? The other salesmen on Jack's list had all been elsewhere the night he died. But one wasn't returning the sheriff's calls, nor was anyone at home when the deputies stopped by there several times. So, where was he?

Dalton noticed several women sobbing into their tissues throughout the crowd, unlike the men who had to suck it up and go on, as if they hadn't lost a good friend, someone they had expected to always be there. And if Ginger's test came back positive? He couldn't even face that possibility. He scanned the crowd again. County officials sat among store clerks, farmers, housewives, and other residents. Dalton's retired third grade teacher appeared to be napping just two pews ahead.

Could one of these people really be a vicious killer?

CHAPTER 17

Ginger zipped through the yellow light, hung a right at the courthouse square, and angled around it to Market Street. One hand steered the small car while the other balanced a double-portioned casserole, a guilt offering for not having visited the Hatfields' home before today.

They should be back from the cemetery by this time. Peggy had looked awful at the funeral, coughing and crying at the same time. Mark had been kept busy comforting her.

A talk with Jack's brother and sister might produce some new information for a different article on his murder. She hadn't been able to interview Peggy before writing the first one. The more publicity the case got, the better the chances of catching Jack's killer.

Maybe she should do another article on abandoned infants as well. It might help smoke out the baby's parents. That would certainly make the job worthwhile. Teenagers or no, the parents needed to be caught and taught a lesson. And it would put Marty Hoggs' snout completely out of joint if her articles helped in that area. The feature editor had always fancied himself far above the other small potato editors.

Ginger parked at the curb, balanced the casserole on her arm, and began the climb up the narrow metal stairway to the Hatfield's apartment.

Mark Hatfield invited her in. Peggy sat drinking coffee at

the old metal kitchen table.

"Can I get you a cup?" Mark asked.

"Sure."

Ginger placed the food on the counter. Mark raised the cover on the casserole dish, took a whiff, and thanked her.

"Sis ain't quite up to snuff yet, what with the funeral and all. I was just about to heat us up some leftovers. This'll be much better."

"It's one of Joe's favorites. I thought you two might like to try it. The heating instructions are on the lid. I put our home phone number on there too, in case you need to contact either of us."

There was a distinct odor in the kitchen. Ginger couldn't quite place it, something like fish or raw liver. The trash certainly needed to be taken out. How difficult their lives must have become.

"Is there anything I can do to help out until you're feeling better, Peggy? I'd be happy to wash up those dishes for you."

"No, I really couldn't expect you to do that. But it's very kind of you to offer. I'm afraid I'm just not used to anyone else working in my kitchen. Mark can take care of things until I'm back on my feet. I just can't seem to get over this."

Ginger wasn't sure if "this" meant Peggy's illness or her brother's death. Probably both. The difference between hearing about how murder affects the surviving family members and actually seeing it first hand was beginning to sink in. Realizing Peggy was still speaking to her, Ginger struggled to catch up to the conversation.

"...your nice article in the paper about Jack. We're grateful that you didn't say anything about our parents' deaths. Mark and I were afraid that would all be dredged up again."

"It didn't seem to be relevant to Jack's death. I thought it best to focus on him, not on your parents." Ginger took a sip of coffee.

"I was wondering if you had thought of anything else that might help find out who killed your brother. Anything at all?"

Mark shook his head.

"I'd like to do another article about him. It might help jog someone else's memory."

"This whole thing just seems like a bad dream. I keep thinking I'll wake up," Peggy said.

"Joe told me that you were going to contact that new lawyer for advice. Was he able to help you?"

"Yes, he's been wonderful," Peggy answered. "We still haven't decided what to do about the store. As soon as I'm able, we'll have to make up our minds. I just can't seem to look that far ahead."

"You know Joe and I will do anything we can to help," Ginger offered. "Would it be all right if I checked back with you in a few days and picked up my dish? We could talk more then. In the meantime, if you think of anything I could use in the article, or if you just need to talk, please give me a call."

Peggy nodded. "There is one odd thing. We haven't heard a peep out of Ruby Miller, and she avoided us at the funeral home. Even though we weren't close, as Jack's girlfriend, I expected better from her."

Interesting. Most women who'd just lost the man they loved would have sought comfort with his family. She'd have to remember to pass this information on to Joe.

"Did she send any flowers?"

"Yes, a huge spray. But she didn't come to the wake either. That seems strange to me. I appreciate you stopping by there last night."

Ginger swallowed the last of her coffee and stood to leave.

"I'm sorry Joe couldn't make it to the wake. He's really busy with the two new cases."

Mark spoke up. "We heard about that baby on the news. Think they'll find the parents?"

"Joe and his staff are doing their best. I'm sure they'll solve both of these cases. I know you're anxious to find out who killed your brother."

She thought about the Hatfields on her way down the stairs. And Ruby Miller. Could any of them be involved in Jack's murder? Why was Ruby acting so odd? Grief? Or something else?

Still on edge from the difficult morning, Ginger needed something to brighten her day. A visit with Debby would make her feel a lot better, she decided, as she made an illegal U-turn and headed toward her daughter's house.

Debby greeted her mother with a big hug and demanded to hear all about her visit to the surgeon. She received a full report while the kettle heated on the stove. Then they settled down to hot spiced tea at the table beside the kitchen window and watched as a pair of cardinals squabbled at the feeder just outside.

"It never ceases to amaze me how tenderly the male feeds the female during the nesting time in the spring, and then ferociously chases her away from the same feeder in the fall." Debby observed.

"You'd think she'd remember that the next time he tried to mate with her and kick him right out of the nest."

Ginger laughed. "There wouldn't be very many new baby birds if that happened."

"I guess you're right. It's a good thing mamma birds do have such a short memory. Sometimes I wish we humans did, too."

"I know. You've had a very rough year." She squeezed her daughter's hand. What else could you say to your child when she had lost hers?

"Yes, I have. But it was tough on you and Dad too. Don't think I haven't realized that." Debby paused for another sip of tea.

"I read your column this morning about the abandoned baby. I'd love to get my hands on the person responsible for that child's death. What you wrote was very moving, Mom. I'm so proud of you."

Ginger couldn't hide a grin. High praise indeed from the young woman who was convinced just a few short years ago that her parents were two dinosaurs who knew diddly.

"That means a lot more to me than you know. It was a difficult piece to write."

Debby glanced out the window. "I'm glad you came by today. There's something I need to talk to you about, and I just haven't quite gotten up the nerve."

Ginger sipped her tea and tried to wait patiently.

"Chuck and I are expecting again. Dr. Lewis says everything looks fine so far, but I'm afraid to even hope. He did an ultra-sound this morning."

Speechless, Ginger hugged her daughter to her. She longed to hold a grandchild again. She prayed that this one would indeed be healthy. The other one had only lived long enough to wrap the entire family around her tiny fingers before dying from severe birth defects.

"Don't tell Dad, okay? I want to tell him myself. Ask him to come by and see me sometime this week. I'm calling Dan tonight to tell him to get ready to be an uncle again." Debby frowned at her cup. "At least he will be if this one is healthy."

"This time everything will be fine, I'm sure of it. Dr. Lewis told us last year that he didn't see any reason why you couldn't have healthy babies, even though there were…difficulties with the first."

Please, let the doctor be right.

"I'll make sure your father comes by soon, so you can tell him. But it is going to be tough to keep this to myself."

Ginger swiped at her watery eyes. Fear, grief, joy. She couldn't remember when she'd had so many different reasons

105

to cry in such a short space of time.

She reached over and ruffled her daughter's hair—thick like her father's and red like her mother's.

"I know. Dr. Lewis told me that too. Guess I'm just a worrywart. That's why I didn't tell you or Dad sooner. Afraid I'd jinx it somehow." Debby's smile crinkled up her freckle-covered nose.

They discussed future ultra-sounds and whether or not Debby and Chuck wanted to know beforehand if the baby was a boy or a girl. Ginger mentally calculated how soon she could start buying baby things. Would she have time enough to enjoy the newcomer? Please, let the biopsy be negative. Joe needed her, her children needed her, and with any luck, so would the new little one.

When the last sip of tea was gone they hugged again, and Ginger put on her jacket to go home.

(HAPTER 18

Dalton was pulling on his jacket when the intercom buzzed. "Fella here to make a statement, Sheriff, about the Hatfield murder. Thought you'd want to talk to him personally."

"Who is it, George?"

"Says his name is Nathan Taylor, tool salesman from Paducah. Says he was with Hatfield the night he died."

"Send him in."

Dalton hung his jacket back on its hook. He'd hoped to get home early for a change, but this interview was too important to delegate to one of his deputies. His hip brushed the desk, and a folder teetering on the top slid to the floor before he could catch it. It was the preliminary autopsy report on Baby Doe.

Jeffords had dropped off the report late that afternoon, and Dalton had taken it with him to another meeting with the state's attorney to discuss both cases. He still had to deal with the mayor and the city council before going home. He'd go over the report with his deputies in the morning.

Taylor entered the room, removed the ball cap covering his wavy hair, and shook Dalton's outstretched hand. He watched Taylor's dark blue eyes dart around the room before the visitor sank into one of the two empty chairs in front of his desk. Dalton leaned back in his own chair, hands together, fingertips forming a steeple.

"That'll be all for now, George." The door shut with a bang.

"I heard about Jack Hatfield's murder today," Taylor began. "Figured I'd better come see you. I had dinner with him the night he died."

"How is it that you're just now hearing about this murder? It's been on all the news reports for miles around."

"My wife had a baby the morning you found Hatfield's body. I've been at the hospital with her and my son ever since."

"And you didn't watch television or read a newspaper at all during that time? Didn't hear the hospital staff or patients discussing it?"

"No. My wife was pretty sick after the delivery, complications from the surgery. We just got home today. We didn't watch television, and we kept the door shut, no visitors."

"How did you find out about Hatfield's death?"

"I happened to catch part of the noon news today and saw something about his funeral. When I realized I was with Hatfield the night he was killed, I figured you'd want to talk to me."

"You're right. We've been trying to reach you for several days. I need to get a statement from you. One of my deputies will take it down, and then you can read and sign it. Okay?"

Dalton reached for the intercom.

"Of course, but I'd like to speak to you in private about something before I make a formal statement, if I may?"

"Sure." Dalton tilted back and listened.

Taylor twisted his cap in his hands and leaned forward.

"My real name is Nathan Taylor Jordan. My father is the man that Hatfield's father shot to death over twenty years ago."

Another survivor of that old murder/suicide. Dalton had never really given much thought to the man who'd died along with Jack's mother and father, or to his family. His sympathy had always been with Jack. This man certainly had reason to hate the Hatfield's.

"My father was a salesman, too. He sold packaged beef out of a freezer truck, door-to-door, to housewives. Burgers, steaks, ribs, stuff like that. That's how he met Mrs. Hatfield. My mother didn't know anything about the affair until he was killed."

"Must have been tough on both of you."

"I was only five at the time. I barely remember my dad. She rarely mentioned him. Most of what I know, I pried out of my uncle."

"Where's your mother now? Still in Metropolis?"

"No. She dropped her married name, took back her maiden name, and moved us over to Paducah. She wasn't well known there. Figured she could get away from the talk that way."

He paused and looked at Dalton as if to see if he was following the story so far.

Dalton nodded, and Taylor continued, "When I first became a salesman, my territory was only in western Kentucky. The southern Illinois salesman retired last year, and I took his area as well."

"But you knew you'd have to sell to Hatfield's Hardware. Didn't that bother you?"

"Nah. I knew Hatfield still operated the hardware store. But neither of us was to blame for what happened to our parents. I figured we could approach the situation like adults. I told him who I was up front."

With Jack dead, who could verify that statement? Mark or Peggy, maybe? It would certainly bear checking out.

Taylor paused, twisting the cap again. His main concern seemed to be whether or not his real identity had to become public knowledge.

"I don't want my wife and child hurt for something my father did, and I don't want to see my mother suffer any more than she already has."

"If it isn't important to the case, then your background won't come out, at least not from this office; but I do need you to repeat it all for the record."

Dalton leaned over again, pressed the intercom button, and told Means to send in a deputy to take down Taylor's statement. When Edwards was seated and ready to write, Taylor repeated his statement to Dalton for him.

"Not long ago the doctor decided to take the baby by Caesarean. When he scheduled my wife's surgery for the day I usually make my rounds in southern Illinois, I called all my customers over here and moved my appointments up a day."

"Is that why you met Jack at a restaurant instead of at the store?"

"Yeah. I explained the situation to him and offered to buy him dinner. I scheduled him last because he was the closest to home."

Dalton interrupted the salesman's flow with another question.

"How did Hatfield seem to you that night?"

"Fine. He was at ease all through dinner, seemed to enjoy himself. He wasn't upset or worried, if that's what you're asking," Taylor replied.

"Go on."

"Hatfield and I met for dinner, discussed business, and he placed an order with me, a nice, big one I might add. Then we just jawed for a while."

"What did you talk about?"

"Well, it was mostly me talking about the baby coming. Probably bored the pants off him. It's our first, you see. I maybe got a little carried away." Taylor smiled.

"What time did the two of you leave the restaurant?"

"Around eight-thirty, I think, maybe a little after. Hatfield finished his coffee, and we left together. He walked me to my truck so I could give him a couple of company freebies. I promised to get the order to him as soon as possible, we shook hands on it, and I left."

"Where did you go after that?"

"I filled my gas tank and got the Popsicles I had promised my wife. She wasn't allowed to eat anything heavy. Then I went straight home. I knew Mary was getting jittery about the delivery."

"How long did it take you to get home?"

Taylor shrugged. "Not long, maybe forty-five minutes or so."

"Who saw you after dinner besides your wife? Will anyone at the gas station remember you?"

Taylor thought a minute.

"I got the gas and Popsicles at the Quick Mart on the south-side Loop in Paducah."

"Did you keep your credit card receipt?"

"I paid cash. Figured I'd turn in a voucher to my boss at the end of the month."

"Would anyone at the store remember you?"

"The clerk was pretty busy; I don't know if he'll remember me or not. I didn't talk to anyone else. Is it important?"

"Right now, I just need to know exactly where everyone involved in the case was at the time of the murder."

And a real close look at this alibi certainly wouldn't hurt. The longer this investigation dragged on, the angrier Dalton felt at Jack's killer. Maybe they had finally gotten a break.

"It looks as if you may have been the last person to see Jack alive. Did he tell you where he was going after he left you? Any idea what his plans were for the rest of the evening?"

"Nope, he didn't mention anything to me. I just assumed he was going home."

"Is there anything else you can tell me? Any reason you know of why someone would want to kill Jack Hatfield?"

"No. And no reason why they would leave his body like that

either. The news report went over how you found him. I almost lost my lunch."

Join the club.

"How well do you know Hatfield's younger brother and sister?" Dalton straightened a paperclip, and wound it around his finger.

"I've seen Mark in the store several times. Don't think he plays with a full deck." Taylor tapped his forehead. "Saw the sister only once. Don't remember her name."

He leaned back in his chair as he thought. "She brought lunch down to her brothers. Didn't say much, seemed shy."

"Anything else you want to add to your statement?" Dalton asked.

"Nope, that's about it."

Taylor had relaxed visibly during the telling of his meeting with Hatfield, Dalton noted. He'd be very interested to know what had made the salesman so nervous about giving his statement.

Dalton stood to indicate that the interview was over.

"Edwards, type that up and have Mr. Jordan read and sign it."

"Make that Taylor, if you don't mind," the salesman responded.

"Mr. Taylor, then."

"Yes, sir. It won't take long, Mr. Taylor. You can have a seat in the reception area, and I'll call you when I'm finished," Edwards said.

"Thank you for coming in. We'll probably be in touch with you again," Dalton said.

Edwards ushered Taylor out of the office toward the visitor area. Dalton took his jacket off the hook again, gave Jenson the assignment of checking out Taylor's story, grabbed the Baby Doe report, and headed for the mayor's office.

CHAPTER 19

Big Ed Simmons watched Larry put the last clean glass under the bar and toss the towel onto his shoulder.

"Time to drink up and head home, folks. We close in ten minutes," the bartender announced to the few patrons left in Pete's Place. A customer in the back raised his glass, and Larry took him one last refill.

Big Ed washed down a sudden taste of anger with a big swallow of cheap beer. Larry never seemed to serve him that quickly or courteously. Acted like putting drinks on the tab was taking money straight out of Larry's own pocket. Everyone knew Big Ed Simmons paid his bar tab, eventually. Besides, the jerk in the back was obviously loaded. It would serve Larry right if the guy had an accident on the way home and the bartender got sued for selling him too much.

"Not going to try to talk me out of another refill, Big Ed?" Larry asked.

He shook his head. "I'm fine."

"You sick or something? According to my calculations you're way below your normal capacity."

"Maybe he's got a hot date," the guy in the back offered.

"With who? Grace Lipinski? He hangs out on her steps an awful lot." Larry chuckled and reached for a broom. "I hear tell she's quite a woman. Even threatened to shoot you, didn't she, Big Ed?"

"Yeah, but her aim is lousy." Big Ed had nursed his drink carefully for some time. Larry was right. He was way under his usual amount, this being only his second. He'd had to make sure it lasted until the bar closed and he left for his meeting. He was too excited to sit at home. Besides, this bar was more like home than that lousy apartment, despite Larry's attitude.

He'd arranged for this meeting to take place at the safest spot he could think of, Grace Lipinski's steps. It would be private, yet near enough to the detention center just in case. If his new client caused any trouble, he'd sing out, and the dear old lady would call the law on him again. The sheriff's office would be his back up.

Too bad Grace Lipinski was such a cranky old biddy. He had never hurt her precious steps, just grabbed a quick nap there sometimes before finding his way home. At least her phone calls to the sheriff usually got him a cup of hot coffee and a free ride.

Her daughter had actually kicked at him once when she came to open the store and found him sleeping there. He'd apologized profusely with a courtly bow, but she'd just glared at him like he was some burglar about to make off with a washer and dryer. Young people these days, no manners whatsoever. Well, she had no idea who she was dealing with.

"Look at him," Larry said to the customer. "Grinning at himself in the mirror like a possum with a fresh persimmon in his paws. You're right. It must be a woman. Who is she, Big Ed?"

He hugged the beer. Better be more careful. He didn't want anyone getting suspicious.

"The only woman in my life is Lady Luck, boys, and I'm still hoping she'll smile on me someday."

"Maybe. She sure hasn't smiled on you before now," Larry responded.

In the mirror, he watched Larry lock the door, turn off the

"OPEN" sign outside the entrance, and place some chairs on top of an empty table.

"Maybe it's that female deputy that came in here asking about him," the customer decided.

"Deputy Peters? Nah, she's got more sense than that." Larry turned to Big Ed.

"She sure was curious about your whereabouts the night of Jack Hatfield's murder, though. Shame I got so busy with a bar full of customers that I didn't have any idea when you left. I'd hate to see you in trouble with the law."

Yeah, Larry, you look worried. Big Ed swallowed the rest of his beer. Wouldn't you just like to know what I really saw the night Jack Hatfield was murdered?

At first he hadn't even realized what he'd seen, just thought it was all part of some murky dream brought on by a little too much of the juice. After he'd left the sheriff's office all sobered up, he'd had time to reflect back on that night. Some of it was still a little foggy, but a careful regimen of drinking and thinking had restored his memory to near normal.

He'd remembered coming to Pete's Place the night of the murder, meeting up with the tourist, and convincing him to buy the drinks. When the drinks and the sucker ran out, he'd tried to get home. The cold wind had made the walk difficult, so he'd sat down for a time in the bushes around the courthouse to rest and warm up.

Someone had driven a truck up to the courthouse, taken a bundle out of the bed, and carried it over to the statue. The dark figure had gotten a ladder from the back stairwell, placed it against the statue, climbed up, and pushed the bundle through the arm. Then he'd climbed back down, put the ladder away, and driven off.

Big Ed couldn't see who it was from behind those ugly bushes, or what it was he'd hung on the statue. He'd thought at the time it must have been one of the city maintenance men setting out the Christmas decorations early. Couldn't understand why they didn't at least wait until after Halloween to begin decorating. Figured next thing, they would be hanging Christmas stuff on the statue by the Fourth of July. At least he had been wrong about that.

After the truck had driven away, he'd settled back into the bushes, intending to make sure the coast stayed clear, and had drifted off into a snooze. When he awoke, he wasn't sure how long he'd been there. Reluctant to get himself arrested for being drunk on county property and risk facing that cranky judge again, he'd crept quietly around the courthouse, out of the bushes, and across the street.

Still unable to navigate home, he'd made his way down Market Street in search of Grace Lipinski's steps. A block or so past her stairwell, he realized he'd missed the mark and worked his way back. He'd sung to himself partly to keep warm and partly because he enjoyed the sound of his own voice.

His thoughts were jerked back into the present by the sound of Larry clinking the few last glasses together in the small sink. Time to go. He threw the last of his change on the counter, patted down his silver hair, and let himself out the door.

He hadn't bothered leaving a tip; wouldn't have even if he'd had the money. Larry would change his tune when the bar tab was paid in full. And Big Ed would be able to treat himself to a real drink, not just cheap beer.

Outside on the street, he pulled his scruffy jacket collar up around his neck, rubbed his hands together to warm them, and started toward Market Street. Maybe he could afford a coat now? Of course, that would depend on how well this meeting went. He let his mind return to mulling over his discovery. What a stroke of luck.

When his memory had cleared a couple of days after the murder, it hadn't taken him long to figure out that the Christmas decorations were actually Jack Hatfield's body. So, of course, the person with the ladder must have been the killer.

He should have told the sheriff what he'd remembered as soon as the mist burned off his brain, but just thinking about it had made him so thirsty, he'd headed straight over to the corner grocery first for a cheap bottle to brace himself. Plenty of time to face the law later. As he'd walked down the street, counting his change, the same truck that had been parked near the courthouse the night of the murder had cruised by. He'd tried to read the license plate and missed seeing who the driver was.

One thing was certain. It wasn't a county vehicle. The sign on the passenger door looked like the kind that belonged to a private business. All he needed to do was find out who drove it that night, and he'd know who had killed Hatfield and placed his body on the statue. That would certainly make Metropolis sit up and take notice.

By the time later arrived, he knew he'd hit pay dirt. A little investigation on his part via a pay phone had uncovered who owned the truck, who usually drove it, and who had probably left Jack Hatfield's body dangling from the arm of the Superman statue.

He reached the corner, pushed the pedestrian button and waited for the light to change.

People in this town thought he'd pickled his brain in alcohol or that he was crazy. Yeah, crazy like a fox. He knew he was still as sharp as the day he'd graduated from law school at the top of his class. He just didn't care about the law anymore, or his family, or much of anything else, except the jolt he got from gambling and the buzz from the booze.

Big Ed could out-think anybody in a little country town that amounted to nothing more than "Smallville, U.S.A." and what he thought now was that he'd finally hit the jackpot. All he'd had to do was figure out how to rake in the prize money, bit by bit. Not enough to make anyone suspicious, just enough to be able to continue his habits without having to rely on his meager disability check every month. Yes siree, that ought to be real easy.

The light changed and he crossed the street, humming to himself.

Even though he'd lost his practice, he was thankful he'd never given the state bar association enough grounds to dump him. He could take the murderer on as a new client. That would assure the client that he would keep all information confidential, and Big Ed, in turn, would be able to request legal fees from said client. Reasonable fees of course, just enough to keep a smart lawyer comfortable. Yep, this was going to be just like shooting fish in a barrel.

He'd come to Pete's Place tonight to swallow a little nerve medicine before the meeting, and to keep from going crazy, staring at the four walls that made up his home. Good thing he was short of money; it wouldn't do to be too foggy to conduct this first official consultation. And he wanted to be sober enough to defend himself in case the killer decided to get rid of his new lawyer like he had Hatfield. Just let him try. He walked the length of the courthouse square's sidewalk, crossed the street, and tossed a salute to Superman on his left. No doubt about it. He'd finally drawn the winning ticket. He covered a belch with his fist.

CHAPTER 20

Early the next morning Linda Peters gritted her teeth and gripped the steering wheel of her car as it crept slowly along Old Marion Road. The cause of her frustration, a large combine that took up her side of the road, and half of the other side as well, as it bumped merrily along in front of her at a not-so-hasty ten miles an hour.

"Terrific. I was hoping I'd missed you this morning."

"Missed who, Mommy?" her daughter asked from the back seat.

Linda glanced in the rear view mirror at eight-year old Pam, playing a hand-held electronic game in the back seat. Toddler Jason, carefully strapped into his car seat beside his older sister, sucked his thumb and sleepily clutched his bunny tightly to his chest while the countryside inched by his window.

"Mr. Farley. He's blocking the road again."

"Can't you pass him? We're already late. I can't miss my bus."

"I could if he were on his tractor and this wasn't a no passing zone. That combine is way to big to pass safely."

Linda checked the side mirror.

"And if you didn't want to miss your bus, you should have gotten out of bed when I called you. And paid attention when you ate your breakfast. We might have beaten Mr. Farley if I hadn't had to mop all that juice up off the floor."

"What about Jason? You had to change his yucky diaper. That wasn't my fault."

"It wasn't really his fault either, honey. Putting food in the top end of a baby only means it's going to come out the other end pretty soon. He's not quite ready to be potty-trained. Grandma says she's working on it."

Linda wished there were some other route to take to work, but all the roads leading into town ran smack through the middle of Massac County's farmland. She often came up behind farmers on their large machinery during the spring and fall and then had to follow them at a very sedate pace.

Fortunately, most farmers she encountered only had a short distance to go before they reached their fields, or they recognized how aggravating it was to follow farm machinery for long distances and would politely pull over onto the shoulder at the first opportunity and wave her around them when it was safe to pass.

Linda knew Jim Farley well enough to know that he was a middle-aged bachelor who'd probably never had to hurry up or wait for anyone else.

Farley owned several pieces of large machinery and hired out daily to work for people all over the area, bouncing along his merry way and frustrating any driver who came up behind him. Linda wondered if he ever did any real farm work or if he just drove up and down the roads all day clogging traffic. No wonder his neighbors all thought he was a pain.

"Can't you do something about Mr. Farley, Mommy? Arrest him, or give him a ticket maybe? If I miss the bus, I won't get to go on the field trip to the pumpkin farm. I want to go."

"Stop whining, young lady. This is your fault as much as Mr. Farley's. I'll drive you to school if we miss the bus, and you'll make the field trip."

Thinking it over, her daughter's suggestion wasn't such a

bad one, if not today, then maybe some time in the future. She'd like to pull that country bumpkin over and give him the lecture of his life. If the noise from the honking horns around her was any indication, the other drivers would cheer her on.

Relieved to see her mother-in-law's driveway at long last, Linda flipped the blinker on and turned in. Before she could get Jason's toddler seat open, B & S bus number thirty-five skidded to a stop at the edge of the driveway and the door flew open. Pam raced around the car and headed for the bus door, calling a greeting to her grandmother as she went.

"Can't you do something about Farley?" the bus driver shouted. "We've been behind him for the last couple of miles and he's made us late. There's no way I can avoid him, he's everywhere at once."

"I'll see what I can do," Linda promised.

"Grandma!" Jason, suddenly wide-awake, practically jumped out of his mother's arms into the eager embrace of Martha Peters.

Seemed like good old Mommy always turned into chopped liver whenever Grandma appeared, and Grandma welcomed time with the children even more than the much-needed income babysitting provided.

It was quite handy having a mother-in-law who lived on one of the main roads into Metropolis, but dropping them off always left Linda with a slightly empty feeling. How many important milestones in her children's lives had she missed while contributing to public safety and the family checkbook?

Jason reached out, took off Grandma's glasses, and tried to put them on his own head. It was one of his favorite games, trying to see the world through her lenses. She gently removed them and pushed them back onto her narrow nose where they belonged.

Linda handed Martha Jason's diaper bag, and deftly removed a piece of plastic Easter grass from his pants. Didn't matter how often you vacuumed the stuff up; Easter grass, like coat hangers, always multiplied when no one was looking.

"Pam won't have any homework to worry about today. Field trip. Jason's ear medicine is in the bag. It needs to be refrigerated."

Martha didn't really need any instructions, but Linda couldn't seem to stop herself from giving them every single morning. "If he starts a fever again, call me, and I'll run out and check him."

Linda leaned over and kissed her son's chubby cheek.

"We'll be just fine. You're the one who needs to take care." The elderly lady peered meaningfully over the thick lenses at her daughter-in-law's ample chest.

"Don't worry, Martha. I've got my vest on, like always."

"Just make sure you keep it on. Can't be too careful, with that murderer running loose. I want you to get him, not the other way around, girl."

Linda smiled at her mother-in-law's concern and got back in the car. She turned around in the big driveway, pulled up to the entrance, and hit the blinker switch. Might as well backtrack a half-mile and detour through a different road to keep from coming up behind Farley again. She could make up some lost time that way.

Waiting for a couple of cars and a tractor to pass by, Linda's mind went briefly over the Hatfield case. She wasn't ready to deal with the murder of the abandoned baby just yet. That one hit too close to home. But something about the Hatfield case had bothered her for the last couple of days. Something wasn't quite right, something she'd either seen or heard.

She glanced in her rear view mirror and waved to Martha and Jason still lingering on the front porch. Suddenly she realized what bothered her. Linda didn't wear glasses but her mother-in-law did, and Martha had pushed them up on her nose just a moment ago.

Mamie Timsley had done the same thing several times during the deputies' interview with her. Martha had the same owl-like appearance Miss Mamie had, with large dark eyes and a head that bobbed about as she tried to focus on anything past her arms.

Miss Mamie had said that she could see into the Hatfield's apartment. She'd insisted she'd seen Mark Hatfield watching television the night his brother Jack was killed, but that she hadn't seen Jack or Peggy.

Bet she couldn't see past her own arms either. Certainly not clear across the street into an apartment window. What did Miss Mamie actually see that night?

Linda pulled out of the driveway and pressed down on the accelerator, eager to get to work and discuss her thoughts with the sheriff.

She'd offer to go back to Miss Mamie's at night and find out what, exactly, was visible from her window. She wanted to make certain Miss Mamie hadn't thought she'd seen Mark Hatfield there because that was what she'd expected to see.

It would probably mean more tea and cookies. Craig would just love that. She'd have to try to sweet talk him into going with her because Miss Mamie seemed to like to feed men and she'd probably open up more with him there.

Two left turns later, Linda was congratulating herself on having out-smarted Farley when she drove out of a curve into a straight stretch and found herself behind the line of cars that slowly followed in his wake. He must have read her mind. Still apparently oblivious to the honks and glares, he continued to bump along; only by now the traffic jam had grown to a number that had to be a county record, even for him.

There was no way she could ever pass all those cars, much less the combine, so she settled back for the long ride into Metropolis.

By the time she reached the city limits, her jaw was stiff from gritting her teeth, her fingers had grown numb from being tapped repeatedly on the steering wheel, but she had come up with a reasonable plan to use the next time she was trapped behind Farley. She would borrow a detachable light from one of the unmarked cars. When she caught Farley holding up traffic for a mile she would pull him over and give him a ticket. There was bound to be something, a taillight, a signal light, some little something that she could nail him over. Forcing him to pry open his seldom used wallet to pay a traffic fine or two just might get his attention.

CHAPTER 21

Deputy Craig Edwards zipped up his jacket and stepped through the sliding glass door onto the wooden deck at the back of his house. The old timers were right. If you didn't like the southern Illinois weather, all you had to do was stick around for a few minutes, and it would change.

There was just enough time to look over the back yard before work.

"Honey, close the door. You're letting all the warm air out," his wife complained from the kitchen.

He slid the door shut and looked over toward the garden. This year's crop had been his best ever. The vegetables his wife had squirreled away would feed them well into next summer. And the roses had been outstanding, in spite of repeated attacks from stray basketballs.

The annual bed near the driveway was completely empty, having done its job for the year. Annuals were fine, but he preferred the perennials that came up every year, like out-of-town friends back for a visit.

"Honey, would you see if there are any tomatoes left? I'm fixing a big salad tonight to go with the pizza," his wife shouted through the kitchen window.

"Yes, dear."

The recent cold snap had sent practically his entire back yard into hibernation. Only one large sturdy tomato plant remained. It still had a couple of large beefsteak tomatoes that neither the cold, his kids, nor the squirrels had been able to damage. He picked the tomatoes and carried them lovingly along in his empty hand to the picnic table near the back door.

He pecked on the kitchen window. "This is the last of them. You'll have to get them from the store next time."

He returned to the tomato bed, set his cup—a freebie from his insurance agent—down, and began to pull up the dead plants. He gathered them up, carried them over to the compost pile at the back corner of the garage, and tossed them in.

Sipping coffee as he went, Edwards wandered over to the other side of the yard, to dead head the last of the rose bed. Except for a few roses and the huge mums alongside the house, most of his flowers were gone for the year.

From now on he'd have to drink his coffee inside at the kitchen table and listen to his wife's chatter while he poured over the seed catalogues and prepared his order for next spring. Not much left to do outside until then. Might as well get the tiller out this weekend and turn the vegetable garden over.

Why on earth, he wondered for the millionth time, hadn't he and his wife moved to Florida—where he could have gardened all year—before they gave birth to their very own basketball team? At least he wouldn't have had to face bleak winter months there.

He turned his mind away from that unhappy thought to the recent murder of Jack Hatfield. They had gone over it and over it at work, and he still couldn't imagine who had put Hatfield on the statue's arm.

He put his empty coffee cup down on the brick border and leaned over to pluck off the dying blooms. Much simpler to grab a boat, take the body out into the Ohio River, and dump it with weights. Craig's hand connected with a thorn.

"Ouch." He sucked on the injured finger, pulled the last dead bloom off, tossed it into the rest of the compost gatherings, and picked them up along with the coffee cup.

"Talking to yourself, Honey? Isn't that a sign of something or other?" his wife called out as she dashed out onto the deck to retrieve the tomatoes.

He ignored her remark and wandered away from the rose bed back toward the house. His yard wasn't large—most of the city's back yards weren't—but he'd managed to make the best use of it. It was all neat, attractive, and in the summer, a feast for the eyes. He sighed over its barrenness now and the long months of waiting until spring.

"You know, honey, it'll soon be time to put up the outdoor lights," his wife reminded him, still shivering on the deck.

"I was wondering if we shouldn't do it really early this year, while the weather holds. You know how you hate doing that job when it's nasty outside. Hmmm? We wouldn't have to turn them on, just get them up."

He glanced up at his house and sighed again. He hated that job; hated taking the Christmas lights down in the cold January weather even worse, but it was easier to just do it than listen to her fuss about it. She'd threatened to let the boys hang the lights one year. He knew he wouldn't have had a single mum or azalea bush left if that had happened.

He loved his wife dearly in spite of the fact that she'd never have the soul of a gardener, and it was much easier to cave in to her blackmail than risk losing one of his precious babies.

"I'll try to get to it Saturday, but I have to till the garden first." Hopefully, just the promise would keep her happy for a few days.

Someone else had been complaining long and loud about early Christmas lights recently. Not a deputy. A prisoner, maybe? No, it had been Big Ed Simmons.

He and Linda had returned to the detention center on the day of Jack Hatfield's murder just as Doody Jenson was escorting Big Ed out. Big Ed was holding forth about the city putting up Christmas decorations too early at the courthouse and how they should wait at least until after Halloween.

He had heartily agreed with the old drunk at the time, but now he wondered what Big Ed had been rambling on about. No decorations had been put up at the courthouse. They usually didn't even arrive there until the week of the Christmas parade late in November.

So why had Big Ed thought they'd been put up when they hadn't?

Was it possible that he'd seen someone around the courthouse the night of Jack Hatfield's murder, even though he'd said in his statement that he'd been asleep and couldn't remember a thing? Could Big Ed have been awake and not realized it, thinking that what he had seen was just a dream?

Could he have just assumed in his condition that it was Christmas decorations when it was really Hatfield's body? Maybe he'd better mention what he'd heard to the sheriff and see if Dalton wanted to trust Big Ed's memory.

A honk in the driveway sent Craig scurrying into the house. He grabbed his gun belt, kissed his wife at the doorway with a force that nearly knocked her down, ran down the front steps, and jumped into the car beside Linda.

He was glad Linda didn't mind picking him up. Riding together gave them a couple of minutes to compare notes on any cases they had been assigned. Today it would give him a chance to try out his theory on her. He wasn't at all happy to hear Linda's latest idea, however.

"I'll go with you to talk to Miss Mamie tonight, but no more tea. The Fig Newtons are out, too. A man has to draw the line somewhere."

He glanced at Linda and watched her smile fall into a frown as he brought up the idea of interviewing Big Ed as well.

"As long as we're out, we might as well go by and see if

he remembers anything more about early Christmas decorations," Craig said.

"I didn't hear him that morning. I went in ahead of you, remember?" She shook her head, ponytail swinging. "I'll go with you, but you'd better stand between us. If Big Ed makes one more crack about the size of my chest, I swear I'll tap his teeth with my nightstick."

Craig nodded, not daring to chuckle out loud at the thought of Linda whacking Big Ed.

CHAPTER 22

The intercom buzzed twice before Dalton managed to reach his desk from the coffee maker.

"Yes, George?"

"Miz Lipinski just called. Says Big Ed is passed out on her steps again. She threw another shoe at him, but he ain't moving. Says if you don't come get him off there, she'll shoot him where he lays.

"Aren't any of the deputies available?"

"She asked for you specifically. No deputies. She wants to file a complaint with you personally."

Dalton sighed. "I'll take care of it, George. Tell her to put the gun away."

He again elbowed his way through the massive glass door, keeping his new coffee cup steady. He would only need one arm to handle Big Ed.

He hadn't gotten around to putting in another request to the maintenance man about the door, but this time he was prepared for the slam. His pants slipped a little lower on his waist as he walked.

Unlike that recent, memorable, early morning, the wind was calm, and no heavy clouds darkened the sky. It was a change he welcomed as he sniffed the crisp fall air.

He glanced at the Superman statue, a new habit since the discovery of his friend's body, and was relieved to see that all was well there.

Would he ever be able to look at the statue without thinking of Jack's death? Of more importance was whether he would ever know the truth about who had put Jack there. The lack of leads in the case really had him frustrated. Dalton crossed the street and approached the stairwell.

His coffee cup slipped out of his hand and smashed on the bottom step as the liquid seeped into his pants. He leaned over and felt Big Ed's neck for a pulse knowing it was too late before he even touched him.

The town drunk lay sprawled there, almost as if he were napping, but a quick look at his face made it obvious to Dalton that this sleep was the permanent one. Big Ed's eyes were wide open as if in surprise, and the back of his head was covered in blood.

Dalton reached for his radio and called for his deputies, this time answering Mean's questions. Sad to say, but none of the early morning scanner eavesdroppers would race to the site at the news of Big Ed's death. Not like they would have for Jack.

While he waited for his deputies to gather equipment and join him outside, Dalton eased himself down onto the bus stop bench located outside the appliance store. He leaned back against the wooden Superman stretched out in flight across the back of the bench.

Who would kill Big Ed, and why? It couldn't have been a robbery. He had little or no money to spend, and always bummed cigarettes and drinks off anyone he could. Folks said Big Ed had pawned everything he could spare in his apartment, except the bed, the couch, and the television.

What other reasons would there be to murder the harmless old drunk? Enemies? Possibly. Big Ed wouldn't have won any popularity contests, but no one seemed to outright hate him.

A random hit? Was the killer stalking anyone he found on Market Street at night? Is that how the deaths were related? The remote possibility of a serial killer roaming Metropolis still haunted Dalton.

Or did the fact that Big Ed was around the square the night Jack was murdered account for two deaths near the statue in such a short time? Was Jack's killer just making sure there were no witnesses? Or could Big Ed have seen something and not told anyone when he gave his statement?

Worse thought: had there been an eyewitness right under Dalton's nose the whole time that he'd dismissed as useless? Had he just lost his only chance to find out who had killed his old friend?

The scariest part of this, Dalton thought, was that these new questions weren't the results of answers from the old.

The detention center door began banging as the deputies headed toward the appliance store.

The deputies secured the scene and were assigned to check the area for evidence while they waited for the crime lab team to arrive from Carbondale. Dalton paced the sidewalk. At last the crime lab team arrived.

"Can't believe we actually beat Jeffords here for once," Jonesy, the head technician told Dalton, as he carefully stepped around Big Ed's body. "Any idea what's holding the good coroner up?"

"George said he had radioed in that he was headed to Big Bay to pick up a body. Sounded like it might be an elderly heart attack victim. He should be on his way back by now."

"Looks like it's none too safe to be out on Market Street at night any more, even this close to your office. If this keeps up, you'll have to declare martial law and call out the National Guard."

Before Dalton could think of a suitably cranky comeback, the head tech turned back to his group and joined a conversation about the changes in the weather.

Jeffords finally arrived and took charge of Big Ed's body amidst jokes from the crime lab team that his wife was going to suspect him of having a girlfriend in Evansville if he didn't stop making so many trips up there with dead bodies. Dalton wasn't amused. Jeffords chuckled and laid out the body bag.

Dalton sat back down on the bench and waited for Jeffords's usual preliminary comments. While he waited, he radioed Means.

"Call Big Ed's landlady and see if she knows how to contact his family. Far as I know, he had none in this area. I just hope they aren't too difficult to locate."

Means grunted a reply.

At least they seemed to have found a weapon this time. A hammer had been discovered under Big Ed's back—the kind of hammer that nearly everyone in Metropolis owned. It was covered in blood and looked to be the right size to have caused the wound. He'd have the deputies check all the local stores that sold any tools, especially Hatfield's. Since Nathan Taylor also sold tools, they would have to take a closer look at him.

Dalton ordered his deputies to check the area around the courthouse again. With the evidence collected, the body removed, and Market Street back to normal, they returned to the detention center.

CHAPTER 23

Dalton called his deputies in for another meeting. He began by giving them an overview of the reports he had received.

"The toxicology report on Jack Hatfield just came in. It confirms that the blood on the ladder was Hatfield's, so that's how the killer got his body over the arm of the Superman statue. The blood we found up there matched Hatfield's as well. We already knew the killer wore tennis shoes. If we can find them, they can be easily identified from the bloody tracks he left."

Dalton shuffled papers.

"There were a few fingerprints on the ladder, most belonging to the janitor. The rest were smudged, indicating the killer wore gloves. The crime lab team found hair and fiber traces all around the statue, but with people walking through there daily, it will be nearly impossible to connect them to anyone. Possible motive: not known at this time."

He moved on to the preliminary report on Baby Doe.

"He was a healthy, full-term baby, no birth defects. He was born alive and bled to death through his umbilical cord, as Jeffords suggested. He'd been dead about three days when Sam Windhorst found him. His footprints were taken at the forensic lab, along with blood and hair samples, but it's still going to be very difficult to identify him unless his parents are located."

Dalton looked up from the report at his deputies. "Any new leads turn up from your investigations?"

Peters answered. "Not a thing. None of the hospitals or doctors reported a suspicious patient."

Doody spoke up. "I called all the motels in the area. None of them found bloody towels, or anything like you'd expect in a birth, and they didn't have any large amount of linens missing either. And no pregnant guests."

"The forensic pathologist confirmed the coroner's original observation that the afterbirth was torn, so it's still very likely that the mother is experiencing great difficulty and needs medical care," Dalton continued.

"Doody, have dispatch contact the area doctors and hospitals again and alert them to keep watching for her. That's our best hope of finding out who the mother is. The blood and hair samples could be used for DNA matching if the parents are ever found. Possible motive: keeping the birth of the child a secret."

Dalton paused for a swig of coffee so the deputies could catch up with their note taking.

"Big Ed's body was just discovered, so of course it will be several hours before the autopsy is complete and we get a preliminary report. The cause of death at first glance appears to be a blow to the back of the head that fractured his skull. The bloody hammer under him appears to be the murder weapon. Possible motive: removal of a potential witness to the Hatfield murder. Or we could have a nut case on our hands."

Wilson spoke up. "You mean someone targeting anyone alone on Market Street at night?"

"Yeah," Dalton responded, "but I hope that isn't it. My gut feeling is that either Big Ed saw something the night Jack died, or the killer thought he did and decided to take him out. I'm pretty certain that the two cases are related, but let's keep an open mind."

Dalton opened the floor to discussion and suggestions from the deputies. Peters shared her idea that Miss Mamie might not really be able to see as well as she had led them to believe.

"I'll go over there tonight and verify what she actually can see in the Hatfield home. And it would be easy to go across the street and interview Hatfield's brother and sister again, see if they have anything new to add to their statements to you."

"Edwards, why don't you go along with Peters? Test your eyesight at Miss Mamie's window."

Dalton didn't want Peters alone on Market Street at night, but he didn't dare say that out loud. She could defend herself as well as any of the male deputies, but why risk it? He'd have sworn that Jack Hatfield could easily have fended off any attackers as well, until recently.

"Yes, sir." Edwards then began laying out his own idea about a possible witness to Hatfield's murder. "Big Ed Simmons was rambling on about Christmas decorations being put up too early at the courthouse the morning Hatfield's body was found. I heard him when we came back from taking statements from the folks who live on Market Street."

"Christmas decorations?"

"Yeah. Figured he was still pretty wiped out so I didn't pay much attention at the time, but now I wonder if he maybe did see something happen at the statue that night and was too drunk to realize it."

Dalton flinched. He had missed something with Big Ed, and now it was too late. How could he have been so blind?

Wilson said, "He might have mentioned his complaint about Christmas decorations to someone else. Or, like you suggested, Sheriff, maybe the killer was afraid Big Ed saw something and decided not to take a chance on his memory."

"I had to head straight for the bathroom that morning when we got back here, thanks to Miss Mamie's tea, so I didn't hear the bit about decorations at the courthouse," Peters put in.

Doody apparently had heard Big Ed's complaints. "But like Craig, I thought he was still pretty smashed and was just rambling." Doody's face turned its usual fiery color, and Dalton knew he was hoping he wasn't in trouble again for not mentioning Big Ed's remarks.

Dalton nodded toward Peters and Edwards. "Find out if the Hatfields have an alibi for last night. We still have to consider them as suspects. My wife visited them recently, and she says that they don't seem to be doing too well. I meant to get by there, but just haven't been able to."

Truth was, he'd been putting off seeing them in the hope that he could find their brother's killer before he had to face them again.

"While you're at it, check all the other residents and see if anyone else might have seen or heard anything last night. That includes Mrs. Lipinski. She said she was too upset to talk to me this morning."

Peters rolled her eyes. "I'm sure Mrs. Lipinski will have plenty to say by tonight."

"She's rarely at a loss for words. Your job this morning is to go to Big Ed's apartment and check it out. Talk to all of his neighbors as well. Edwards, check on Big Ed's whereabouts last night. You might start at Pete's Place, he hung out there a lot."

Dalton turned to the other deputies. "Doody, you talk to Ruby Miller again. Find out if she has an alibi for last night. From what Peggy told Ginger and me, Ruby's been acting really odd lately."

Billy and Doody exchanged looks.

"Wilson, you check out the tool salesman. Find out what he was doing."

Dalton wondered what the looks meant. They obviously had something on their minds. He shrugged mentally; they'd tell him when they were ready.

Dalton got up to get another cup of coffee, a sign that the meeting was over.

Doody Jenson stood up to leave, turned around at the door, hiked up his own pants, and said, "You know, Sheriff, in mystery books, it's usually the person who finds the body that turns out to be the killer. You're starting to find a lot of bodies lately."

The deputies looked at Dalton as if to gauge his reaction to Doody's ill-timed joke. Feeling the weight of his own stupidity, Dalton decided not to chew Doody up and spit him out for once.

"Yeah, but I sure couldn't have carried Jack's body up the ladder and placed it on the statue without losing my dinner. Those courthouse bushes come in real handy sometimes, don't they?"

Doody blushed. Peters and Edwards chuckled on their way out of the office with him close behind them. Wilson stayed in his seat.

"Sheriff, I need to talk to you about the Hatfield case in private," he began.

Dalton dropped back into his chair. "Sure. You got some idea of your own to share about who killed Jack Hatfield?"

"Nope. Just some solid evidence about who didn't," he replied.

Wilson leaned forward and unburdened his conscience, giving details and background of his affair with Ruby Miller and their alibi the night of the murder.

Dalton listened impatiently to the story. He felt sorry for Wilson, for the home life he'd endured. But that didn't change the fact that he was having an affair with a suspect in a murder case and had turned in a false statement from her to keep the affair a secret.

Much as he hated to do it, he'd have to suspend Wilson

until he learned his lesson and got his personal life back on track. He might even have to fire him.

"And you are not to see Ruby Miller until this investigation is over, even if it takes years." Dalton felt his blood pressure jump several points. "Call her and tell her that. Nothing else about the case, understand?"

"Yes, sir."

Dalton knew Wilson understood very well that he would be lucky to keep his job. Wilson left Dalton's office, passing Doody, who was hovering in the hallway, apparently listening for and dreading the explosion. Dalton watched as Wilson gave Doody a friendly thwump on the back, gathered up his things, and headed out the door. So Doody had probably known something about the affair and had kept it quiet.

"Come back into my office for a minute, Doody."

"Yes, sir."

"Close the door."

Jenson closed the door and stood at attention in front of Dalton's desk, looking like a prisoner before a firing squad.

"I know you and Wilson are close. I can't afford to suspend another officer right now, so I won't even bother asking you how much you did or didn't know about his private life."

Dalton watched Jenson swallow hard. He had known, all right.

"We have too many cases to work on for me to lose you, too. Just remember this, anyone who hampers an investigation in this office by withholding information is headed straight for a suspension or firing, depending on my mood. Got it?"

"Yes, sir." Sweat trickled down Jenson's face.

"I'll talk to Ruby Miller myself. That way, I'll know I'm getting first hand information. You take Wilson's assignment with the tool salesman. That's all for now."

Doody Jenson beat a hasty retreat out the office door.

(HAPTER 24

Ruby Miller leaned against the screen door of her small front porch and sniffed at the smell of the nearby river. A honk from a tugboat on the far side drifted across to her.

She was attempting to entice her cat to leave its favorite lounging spot and come outside when the sheriff pulled into her driveway. Her stomach felt as heavy as her old bowling ball. She wished she didn't have to face him.

She offered Dalton a seat on the couch and chose the chair across from him for herself. She folded her hands tightly in her lap and tried to look casual. The late-afternoon sun streamed in through the window on her left, giving her ample light to read his face by. Ruby could easily see the anger in his face. She hoped he couldn't see the uneasiness in hers.

The calico cat that had been lazing in the sunny window jumped down and approached Dalton, cautiously sniffing out the stranger in her territory. Dalton gave her a friendly pat, and she flopped down on the sheriff's boots, and began to purr.

"I suppose you know I came here to talk to you about Jack's murder and the false statement you turned in about where you were the night he died? I assume Deputy Wilson told you about our conversation this afternoon?"

Ruby nodded. "Billy called me when he got home. Barb and the girls were gone, so he was able to speak freely. He told me about what happened in your office."

This was so embarrassing. What could she say?

"I'm sorry, Sheriff, for lying about being alone on the night of Jack's death. I knew neither Billy nor I was guilty and that we had witnesses, if we needed them. I didn't think it would make much difference to your case. I didn't lie for myself, you understand, but for him."

"Of course it made a difference, Ruby."

"I didn't really think about that. I just wanted to protect Billy. If his marriage should break up, I want it to be his choice, not because it was forced on him; and certainly not by me. He must care for me a little too, or he wouldn't have spoken up and given me an alibi."

She paused, hoping he would confirm her reasoning about the situation. He didn't.

"Even though you weren't involved in the murder, Ruby, I needed to know that. I could've checked it out, scratched you off the list of suspects, and moved on to someone else. You and Billy hindered our investigation of a major crime."

His voice rose as he spoke, and the cat got up and dashed under her mistress's chair to watch from behind Ruby's feet.

"I can understand you to some degree, but not him. He's going to have to work very hard to get himself back on my team."

Ruby leaned over and lifted the cat to her lap. Billy, lose his job because of their affair? He loved being a deputy. That would sink their relationship quicker than anything except maybe losing his kids. She snuggled the cat to her chest, suddenly feeling cold in spite of the warm sun.

"How were things between you and Jack, Ruby? I thought you two were pretty committed. How is it that you were seeing someone else? And why didn't you break it off with one of them?"

She cringed at the barrage of questions. How could she

explain without telling him everything?

"Our relationship started out well enough, Jack's and mine that is. He made it pretty clear from the start that he wasn't interested in getting married, ever. His parents' marriage had soured him on that idea, and he had Peggy and Mark to care for."

The cat wiggled free from Ruby's tight grip, and curled up on her lap. She gently scratched the cat's ears.

"How did you feel about that? Didn't it bother you?"

"No. And I didn't want to move in there with them. Jack agreed. He said it would upset them both too much. We decided to leave well enough alone. He'd stay the night with me from time to time, but we wouldn't tie each other down to anything more permanent."

She pushed a stray strand of hair off her forehead.

"I was still smarting from my divorce and was in no hurry to get remarried or even live full time with someone. The arrangement suited us both just fine. Over time we settled into a routine, and I honestly thought I was happy with that."

The cat batted Ruby's hand to encourage more scratching, and was quickly placed back under the chair for her trouble.

"Weren't you?"

"I didn't give it much thought. Then about a couple of months ago Jack began to change, I mean really change. He became quiet, moody, distracted—nothing like the friendly, outgoing man I had known for so long."

The man she thought she knew. How well did people ever really know each other?

"Mark and Peggy said the same thing. Any idea what made him change?"

"I asked him about it, but he wouldn't tell me what was wrong. I thought maybe the business was in trouble, that he was afraid of losing it. A lot of small-town, family-owned stores do go under." She shifted in the chair again. Should she say more?

"He got angry whenever I brought up the subject, so I dropped it. The last month or so before his death I didn't see him quite as often. He suddenly got very busy and sometimes canceled dates with me."

Nothing else seemed to relate to Jack's murder. Best to say as little as possible and not cause more problems for herself.

"As to why I didn't break it off with one of them, what can I say?" she shrugged. "I wanted to break it off with Jack. I knew I'd fallen in love with Billy and that it wasn't fair to string Jack along if it was over."

In all honesty, she hadn't thought Billy would leave his wife for her and was afraid to push the issue.

"I didn't feel very good about what I was doing, but I told myself I would be dumping Jack just when he needed me. And I was afraid he might wonder why I called it off after all this time."

"Afraid? Why?"

"He might've decided to do some checking and found out about Billy. It would've seemed like history repeating itself to Jack, like I was treating him the way his mother treated his father. He took their deaths very hard, harder than most people realized."

"It was pretty tough on him. Jack had to grow up overnight. None of us had the slightest idea how to help."

"I didn't want to hurt him like that, and I didn't want to take a chance on getting Billy into trouble. Not very courageous, I suppose, but a woman in love does a lot of dumb things."

"Could Jack have had another woman?" Dalton asked.

"I thought of that, but in a town this size, things like that usually get out unless you're really careful."

She blushed remembering how her own care had not kept

her affair with Billy from being discovered. And yet, in spite of what she'd just told the sheriff wasn't this what she'd secretly been hoping for? That someone would catch them together and bring the affair out into the open? That Billy would be forced to tell his wife what was going on and let the chips fall where they may? And hadn't she been praying that they'd fall in her direction?

"So you have no idea what brought about the change in Jack?"

She shook her head. "None whatsoever. I'm certain there wasn't another woman. He didn't seem like a man with a new romance. He just seemed anxious and worried—very worried."

She tucked her foot under her leg and leaned back in the chair. "Maybe if you solve this case, you'll find out what was wrong."

Dalton scratched his neck with the tip of his pen. "Only if it's tied to the murder. Otherwise, we'll probably never know."

He stood up to leave. "You understand that it's very important for Billy not to see you while he's on suspension? He has to get his private life together. He can't let it interfere with his work any more. If he does, he'll lose his job."

She nodded and saw him to the front door.

The cat streaked outside, past Dalton, and up the nearest small dogwood tree, then sat down on a low limb, and watched the visitor leave. She would scratch on the front screen when she wanted back inside.

Ruby closed the door and paced the living room restlessly. Was Barb home yet? Was Billy telling her now? How would she take the news? Would she throw him out? Or would she hang on and try to save her marriage for the sake of the children? Why didn't the phone ring? What would she do if she lost Billy?

A purposeful scratching at the door interrupted her worries.

CHAPTER 25

When he saw his wife pull into the driveway, Billy went outside to help her and the girls carry in the groceries. They lined all the sacks up neatly on the counter between the kitchen and dining area, and then he turned to the girls.

"Heather, take Patty downstairs and watch TV for a while. I have something important to discuss with your mother."

Heather gave her father a questioning look.

"Go on."

He watched them go down the stairway and then turned to his wife.

Barb busied herself with putting away the groceries. She liked things a certain way, so he folded his arms against his chest, leaned against the sink giving her room to work, and began to talk.

"I've been suspended from my job, Barb. Sheriff Dalton told me to come home and straighten out my personal life. And that's exactly what I intend to do. I'm tired of living this way, in a marriage that isn't a real marriage."

She put the milk in the refrigerator, shut the door, and walked back to the counter, barely giving him a glance.

"I wondered why you came home so early today. Why would he suspend you? Our marriage is our business and no one else's, and that includes your boss. The sheriff has no right to interfere in our private lives."

She reached for a box of crackers and a sack of cookies to put in the pantry.

Billy shifted his weight to the other foot. "I'm going to lay all my cards on the table. What you do about the situation is up to you. I already know what I'm going to do. Things have got to change around here."

He swallowed hard. "I'm sorry, Barb. I wish I didn't have to say this. I've gotten myself involved with another woman. I'd rather not say who it is. Dalton found out and suspended me because he felt it interfered with my job."

She stopped unloading the groceries, giving him her full attention.

"This is the only time I've ever even looked at anyone but you. I didn't mean to now. It just happened. I'm not excusing myself. I shouldn't have done it."

"You bet your badge you shouldn't have done it."

"I didn't want to hurt you, or the kids, or her, but this has made me wake up. I can't live in this marriage any more. If you want out because of this I'll understand, but if you want to save our marriage then we're going to have to get some counseling."

"You're having the affair, and you want me to get counseling? That's a laugh."

"You can't have everything your way. There has to be some compromise. I don't even feel like a man any more."

"I told you what I would do if you ever tried to leave me. Now you've given me just exactly what I need to do it." She slammed a large juice can down on the counter.

"I know you're hurt and angry. I don't blame you. What I did was wrong. I should've insisted we straighten this out sooner, instead of letting things slide."

"There is nothing to straighten out. Don't blame me for your sick, animal ways."

"You're the one that's sick, Barb. Married people aren't

supposed to live together like brother and sister; they're supposed to live like people in love. You haven't shown me any love in years."

"There is nothing wrong with me," she said through gritted teeth. "All you think about is sex. Well, after this I won't have to put up with it. As far as I'm concerned, this marriage is over." She stalked back to the pantry and put away the juice can.

Billy shook his head. "I've only stayed for the kids. If it hadn't been for them, I would've left a long time ago."

"Well, don't let them stop you. You know where the door is. The girls and I will be just fine."

"Look, I can't change the fact that I was unfaithful, any more than you can change the fact that you've never been a real wife to me. But we could get counseling, find a way to forgive each other, and get on with our lives, for their sakes. I'm willing to try if you are."

"There's nothing wrong with me, and I don't plan to change my life!" she shouted. "As for you, I've always said you could leave any time you wanted, as long as you were prepared for the consequences. I'm not going in for counseling and opening my private life to some stranger; so you just pack your things and get out—now!"

It looked like he'd have to make some threats of his own for a change.

"If that's how you want it, that's fine. I'll go stay at my mom's. But you'd better understand one thing. I am taking the kids with me. And when we get the divorce, I plan to ask for full custody."

"You'll never get it. This whole town thinks I'm Super Mom."

"Don't bet on it. I am not going to let you turn those girls into a chunk of ice like you. It's one thing for you to ruin my life. I'm not going to let you ruin theirs."

147

She grabbed the nearest thing at hand—a large pickle jar—and threw it at him. He ducked, and it crashed against the counter spewing pickles and juice all over the cabinets and dripping onto the highly polished floor.

"I won't let you make our private lives public!" she shouted. "I'll swear you abused me!"

"That threat won't keep me in line any more, Barb. You have no proof, because there never was any abuse. If you lie to the judge, you'll go to jail. Think about that."

Heather ran up the basement stairs and froze in the doorway. Patty was right behind her.

"It's okay, girls. It was just an accident. Go back downstairs with your sister, Heather, and stay there until I call you."

His girls rarely saw their parents fight, had rarely even heard them talk to each other lately. He knew they must both be frightened.

Barb turned and ran out of the kitchen and into the bedroom, slamming the door behind her. He had never known her to lose her temper like that in front of anyone. Not even her family. She had always kept a tight lid on her feelings.

He picked up the pickles and glass pieces while Heather found a towel and began to mop up the juice. Patty, too young to understand, stood in the doorway and cried.

He didn't have the heart to insist that the girls go downstairs again by themselves. When the mess had been cleaned up, he went to the bedroom door.

"Barb, I don't blame you for being angry, but you have to accept at least part of the blame for the failure of this marriage. Think about it."

No answer.

"We'll be at my mom's until I hear from you. Believe me, I meant what I said. If you insist on us splitting up, I'll file for divorce and ask for custody of the girls. I'll also demand that you see a court-appointed psychiatrist, and the real truth about our relationship will come out."

He paused again and waited for a reaction from her. None came.

"You know as well as I do, how we live isn't normal. I think a judge will agree with me. The decision is up to you; whatever happens, the kids and I are not going to live like this another minute."

He didn't know if he could actually force her to see a psychiatrist, but the threat just might scare her into doing something positive for a change. He'd reached the breaking point and was willing to do whatever he had to in order to get something that resembled a normal family life.

By now both girls stood behind him in the hallway, listening. Heather held Patty's hand while they both cried. He hugged them close, and then took them into their room to help them pack.

An hour later, the three of them got into his truck and left for his mother's house. Barb hadn't come out of her room, but he had heard her crying through the door. Billy was scared, but he felt better than he had in years.

CHAPTER 26

Linda Peters watched Craig Edwards slouch down the stairway and into his living room to find his sister-in-law lighting candles and arranging baskets of all sizes on a card table hidden by a lace tablecloth. He stood in the doorway with his mouth hanging open until his wife came in from the kitchen loaded down with a tray of hot hors d'oeuvres and gently pushed him out of her way.

"What's going on, Diana?"

"Honey, I told you last night I was having a basket party to help my sister get started in this business. And it'll help me too. If she makes a good sale, I'll get some things for free—and I love these pretty little handmade baskets."

Edwards frowned. Having just placed an order, Linda knew those "pretty little baskets" were also pretty expensive. She was sure her fellow deputy was calculating whether or not his paycheck had just disappeared before his very eyes.

"You didn't mention any basket party to me," he fumed. "Lucky for me Peters is here to pick me up. We have to re-interview some witnesses downtown. What if I hadn't had to work? What would I have done with myself while you girls ate and talked baskets?"

"You would've gone to the basement with the boys, eaten pizza, and played games," she returned. "And I did tell you, but you had your head stuck in a seed catalogue as usual and didn't hear me. I'll save some pizza for you in the fridge. We should be done by the time you get home anyway, so don't panic."

Diana nibbled on a cheese cracker and held the platter in front of Linda for a sample.

"Try this, it's a new cheese ball recipe. Got it out of a magazine."

"Thanks. Could you write it down for me? I've got a family reunion next week. Always looking for something new to take." Linda put a few snacks on a napkin and headed toward the door.

"Sure thing. See if you can cheer Craig up a little while you're out." Diana turned to her husband.

"Close your mouth, honey. You look like a fresh catfish just hauled up on the river bank."

"Problem?" his co-worker innocently inquired, as she carefully backed the car out of the driveway.

"Basket parties," he huffed, wrestling the seatbelt into place. "Don't grown women have anything better to do than eat and look at baskets?"

Linda had been invited to the party, but had declined due to work. She had still given Diana an order that had made her eyes light up. She decided not to share that information with Craig.

She drove them to Market Street and parked on Seventh, beside Hatfield's Hardware Store. Stepping out of her car, she glanced up at the old building and wondered what it was like for the Hatfield family to have lived downtown all their lives.

They'd never had a yard with trees or plants to enjoy. She didn't think she could survive like that. She guessed by the way he looked at the brick and concrete that Craig had the same thoughts as they clanged their way up the stairs.

Brother and sister sat in the kitchen finishing up dinner,

burgers from the nearby Dairy Queen. Linda sat down at the table with them, and Craig leaned against the sink.

Judging from what the sheriff had told them, the kitchen was obviously no cleaner than when his wife had visited, and Linda noted that it smelled as if the trash hadn't been carried out in quite sometime.

She began the questioning. "Sheriff Dalton wanted us to check in with you again. We located the tool salesman who was with your brother on the night he was murdered. Do either of you know him? His name is Nathan Taylor."

Mark shrugged and answered first. "I seen him in the store a few times. Seems like a nice enough guy."

Peggy shook her head.

"Taylor told the sheriff he met you in the store once, Miss Hatfield," Craig chimed in.

She shook her head again. "I remember meeting some salesman. I don't remember his name." Her voice was deeper than usual, as if she had a sore throat, and she was seized with a sudden coughing fit. Mark got up and got her a glass of water.

"Guess the damp weather has gotten to me." She took a drink of the water and gave her brother a grateful look.

"Can you think of any reason Taylor might have had to kill your brother?" Craig asked.

They looked surprised and both shook their heads.

"And you're sure you don't know him aside from the business?" Linda asked.

Mark and Peggy shook their heads again.

"Nathan Taylor's father was the man your father shot to death some twenty years ago. Are you sure Jack didn't tell you about him?" Craig demanded.

Both siblings' jaws dropped in surprise. "Jack never said a word to me or to Mark. Mark would've told me," Peggy said.

Mark nodded in agreement.

152

"Do you think he killed Jack?" Peggy asked.

"He was the last one to see your brother alive, as far as we can tell. One of our deputies is checking out his alibi for the time after he says they parted. If either of you remember anything about him, it could be very important," Craig answered.

"Have you thought of anything new to tell us about your brother?" Linda picked up the questioning. "Have you been able to discover why he was down or distracted before his death?"

"Not unless it had to do with the business." Peggy cleared her throat again. "And, as I told Joe, he never discussed business with us."

"Have you decided what to do now, with your brother gone?" Linda inquired gently.

Mark answered the question. "Neither of us knows how to run the business, so we're thinking of selling it, if we can find someone who'll let us stay here in the apartment as part of the deal. Never lived anywhere else. Wouldn't know where to go," he finished.

"We can't seem to find anyone who's interested in managing the store, because we can't afford to pay much. Thankfully, Jack did leave a little insurance," Peggy put in. "That young lawyer the sheriff recommended called yesterday to let us know. He said it wasn't a large amount but that it should take care of us for a while. Could you pass that along to Joe?"

Linda nodded.

Craig jumped back in. "Did either of you know Big Ed Simmons?"

"Sure. He hung around the store some, usually trying to sell Jack some old stuff he had, probably to raise drink money. Jack sometimes bought the stuff just to get rid of him," Mark answered.

Peggy said, "We saw on the noon news that he was killed, but they didn't give many details." She shivered. "Do you think

153

his death is somehow related to Jack's?"

"We don't know for certain what the motive was yet. If it turns out to be related, we'll let you know. Could you tell us where you both were last night between midnight and dawn?" Linda asked.

"We were right here," Mark answered. "Never go out at night."

"Can anyone else verify that?"

"There's no one here but the two of us. We never have company," Peggy answered.

"Did you see or hear anything unusual down on the street last night?" Linda asked.

"Walls are too thick to hear much of anything going on downstairs," Mark answered.

"Why would we want to kill Big Ed Simmons?" Peggy asked. "We barely knew him."

"As I said, we don't know why he was killed, Miss Hatfield," Linda responded as she stood up to leave. "We need to talk to the other neighbors. We'll be in touch if we learn anything new about your brother's death."

Craig turned to Mark. "I know the sheriff checked the store's inventory with you the day your brother died, but he wants us to double-check it. Would you be willing to let us take care of that tonight? If not, we can get a search warrant and come back tomorrow. We'll also want to check your tool chest up here."

Mark looked at Peggy and she nodded.

"Won't be necessary. You're welcome to look tonight. Jack kept the list in the file cabinet downstairs. Like I told the sheriff, I don't keep a tool chest up here. Always grab whatever I need from downstairs to fix anything."

Mark took his jacket off the back of the kitchen chair and led the way downstairs.

An hour later the two deputies stood outside on the street

and exchanged thoughts.

"Whew, the sheriff was right. They aren't coping well," Linda began. "That apartment is a mess, and the smell is awful."

"Guess it's true, they can't get along by themselves," Edwards agreed. "Don't know what they'll do now. They haven't even had the store open since their brother died. At least that made our job easy. Inventory list and stock all matched, nothing missing."

He looked both ways before crossing Market Street, even though it was completely deserted. Linda double-timed to keep up with his long gait.

"I don't see anyone buying the business and letting them live in the apartment above, do you?"

Craig's only response was a shrug.

CHAPTER 27

Linda didn't have to ask if Mamie Timsley had heard the news of Big Ed's death. She was obviously prepared for their visit. Instead of plying them with stale Fig Newtons, she offered fresh coconut cake. It was warm and delicious, and Craig quickly dropped into the chair Miss Mamie offered and waited expectantly. Out came the teapot and cups again.

Linda joined them at the table. She swallowed her piece of cake and got down to business.

"Miss Mamie, did you see or hear anything unusual downstairs last night? Anything at all?"

"No," she said thoughtfully. "Just Big Ed Simmons singing, like always. Guess he won't be doing that anymore."

"What time was that?"

"Pretty late, I think. I got up to go to the bathroom about one, and it was well after that," she responded.

"Did you happen to look over at the Hatfields' last night?" Linda asked.

"Why, yes. They were both in the living room all evening." Her thin, white eyebrows shot up. "Why are you asking about Mark and Peggy? You don't suspect either of those children do you? Why, I don't believe either of them could hurt a fly."

"We have to check on everyone, Miss Mamie, before we can figure out who the guilty person is," Craig said between bites.

Leaving him chewing happily, Linda strolled over to the window, stood to one side, and looked into the Hatfields' apartment. The lights were on and someone was sitting in the living room. She called Miss Mamie over to the window and asked her to describe what she could see.

"Well, I see Mark sitting on the couch with his feet up, like always. Peggy is just coming out of the dining room, heading for her chair. They always sit in the same place," she said.

"How do you know which one is which, Miss Mamie? They're both about the same height and weight," Linda pointed out.

"Not really. Peggy's a little heavier than Mark. Poor thing has put on quite a bit of weight this year. She doesn't exercise enough, you know." Miss Mamie squinted and leaned toward the window for a better look.

"My, she must be taking Jack's death hard. That shirt used to be too tight, now it's hanging on her. Poor thing, must be grieving too much to eat. Anyways," she continued, "Mark is wearing his hat. He rarely takes it off." She smiled, as if pleased at her own powers of observation.

Linda thought a minute. "The night Jack Hatfield died, you said Mark was watching TV and Peggy wasn't in the room. How do you know it wasn't the other way around?"

"Easy again." She adjusted her glasses. "The night Jack was murdered, Mark was sitting on the couch nearly all evening with his feet up on one end, like now. Had his hat on, too. Peggy's chair was empty all evening, so she must have been in bed with a headache."

"Did you see Mark leave the living room at any time?" Linda asked, glancing over at Craig; he was busily scraping up crumbs and trying to take down Miss Mamie's statement at the same time.

Miss Mamie thought a minute. "No, I didn't see him leave, but I looked over once and no one was there. Didn't I say that before when you were here? I don't think he was gone more than a couple of minutes, and then he came back and sat down. Never did see Peggy. Is that important?"

"Probably not, Miss Mamie, but we do appreciate all your help."

Linda thumped Craig on the arm. "Let's go, Craig." She wanted to get the other interviews done and get home to her family, but suspected that Craig was in no hurry to go back to a house full of females.

"We'll let you know if we need anything else," Linda said from the back doorway. She paused there while Craig reluctantly put down his plate, took a wistful glance at the rest of the cake, and followed her to the door.

The last stop for the deputies was Grace Lipinski's home. The elderly woman picked up the remote, pressed the mute button, and carefully tucked a magazine down into the basket beside her chair.

"I know the sheriff spoke with you and your daughter this morning, but he asked us to check in on you tonight to see if you remembered anything else," Linda began.

"No. I told the sheriff everything I knew this morning. I heard a noise downstairs, like someone yelling. I looked outside and saw Big Ed lying there. I thought he'd passed out again, so I threw another shoe at him." She sniffed. "It bounced right off his shoulder. I figured he was dead drunk. I never dreamed he was really dead. Serves him right, though. He hasn't been much use to anybody in years. At least I won't have to put up with his racket now."

Linda hoped she didn't turn as sour as Mrs. Lipinski was if she lived to old age. She much preferred her mother-in-law's positive attitude toward life.

"Do you know if Big Ed had any enemies, Mrs. Lipinski?"

"Probably half this town. Certainly anybody who lives on Market Street. He drove us all crazy with his middle-of-the-night carryings-on."

The old lady was obviously on a roll now. Linda could almost guess what was next.

"I remember when he was a young man, just starting his law practice. So much promise, and he just threw it all away. Lost his family and friends, too. I just do not understand how a man can let that happen to himself."

Just what Linda had expected to hear. "When you looked down the stairs, did you see anyone else there with Mr. Simmons?"

"No. Just him lying there for all the world to see. So embarrassing to have that drunk hanging on my doorstep all the time. It's entirely your fault. If you people had done your jobs and kept him in jail, this wouldn't have happened. He would still be alive."

Linda didn't dignify that with an answer. "The sheriff said you heard Mr. Simmons call out. Did you hear anyone else down there?"

"No, only him. I waited a while, looked out again, and he was still there. That's when I called your office. Like I said, you people should have kept that old troublemaker in jail after the last time I called. I plan on giving the sheriff a piece of my mind next time I see him. I was too upset this morning."

Lucky for the sheriff. Seeing she had no more information to give, Linda thanked her, and the deputies took their leave.

Linda dropped Craig off at home. She watched him slink around to the back of his own house, like a wary burglar on the alert for danger and knew he was going to try to sneak, unseen, in the back door of the kitchen and down the basement stairs to join his sons in their all male refuge.

Linda headed home to tuck the kids in for the night and put her feet up for a few minutes. She was convinced that the alibi Miss Mamie had provided for Mark wouldn't hold up. Peggy could just as easily have worn his clothes and hat and sat on the couch, and Miss Mamie wouldn't have known the difference.

Her own eyesight was much sharper than that of the elderly woman's, and she couldn't distinguish between brother and sister from across the street either, except by Mark's cap and where they sat.

What Linda couldn't figure out was why either Mark or Peggy would want to kill their brother. They obviously weren't doing well without him.

Still, she couldn't wait to tell her boss what she and Craig had learned, come morning. She was pleased that they did have something to tell him and wondered if Doody had come up with anything in his investigation.

She liked Doody, but sometimes his ultra-conservative views grated on her nerves. She liked Billy, too, and was sorry to hear about his suspension. And Billy was the sharp one of the group, always a step ahead of the rest of the deputies. Maybe, just this once, she and Craig would find the answers first. Wouldn't that be something?

The sound of her husband snoring on the couch as she walked in made her realize it was way past their bedtime. She tapped him on the arm, a tad gentler than she had been with Craig earlier, and guided his sleepy body to the bedroom.

(HAPTER 28

Doody drove over to the steak house where Hatfield and Taylor had eaten the night Hatfield died. A game of phone tag with Taylor's voicemail earlier in the day had produced zero results.

With Billy suspended, he'd have to tackle the salesman at home, and he was eager to get to it. He wanted to show Dalton that he could hold up his end of the trolling net, even without Billy—tough as that would be. He would have dinner and ask again about the night Hatfield and Taylor were there. Then he would head across one of the bridges to Paducah and check out Nathan Taylor's alibi.

The restaurant was full, so he parked himself at a table with two local truck drivers and a farmer. They were all curious to know what was being done to solve the recent flood of murder cases. He'd been with the sheriff's office long enough to know how to give answers to civilians without really saying anything.

Doody got the rib eye special, gulped it down, asked for his bill, and prepared to leave. While the regular night waitress rang up his bill, he asked her if she'd seen Hatfield and Taylor at the restaurant the night Hatfield died.

"Sure, I waited on them. They seemed to enjoy the meal and left me a nice tip," she responded.

"Do you know what time it was when they left?"

She leaned on the counter and popped her chewing gum while she thought. "There was a problem in the kitchen with one of my orders. By the time I got it straightened out, they'd left. Someone else must have rung up the bill. I'd say it was about eight-thirty."

Doody thanked the waitress and left. He pointed his car down Highway 45 toward the Irvin Cobb Bridge at the edge of Brookport. That bridge would bring him into Paducah at the west end of town. From there he could follow the Loop around the edge of Paducah to the Reidland area, the suburb where Taylor and his family lived. The trip would take him about thirty minutes.

Doody never understood why so many drivers were nervous about crossing the old Irvin Cobb Bridge. Just because it swayed in the wind, that was nothing to panic over, although the bumpy metal deck did make it tricky for folks with new tires. Still, it was beyond him why residents on both sides of the river usually chose the modern, four-lane I-24 Bridge at the edge of Metropolis instead, ignoring the fact that it was closed far more often for repairs than its old bright blue neighbor just a couple of miles upriver.

The river was still choppy and full of debris from the recent heavy rains. Several barges were parked in a string at the river's edge, waiting to lock through.

Doody hummed around the Loop, carefully watching for the changing speed limits. By the time he arrived at the Taylor home, he was beginning to feel nervous. He wasted several minutes hunting for his notepad and pen and then spent some time looking around the neighborhood.

The Taylor home was situated in the middle of a cookie cutter subdivision, surrounded by houses that were distinguishable from each other only by color and landscaping and the amount of bicycles, wagons, toys, and barking dogs in the yard. He watched as a mother came out her front door across the street and called her children in for the evening, breaking up a game of hide-and-seek. Doody wondered sadly if his yard would ever look that messy and well worn.

He made himself get out of the car and go up to the door. He was slightly hesitant because he knew the Taylors had a baby, and he didn't want to upset the new mother.

She answered the door, baby on one arm, bath towel on the other, checked his identification, and invited him in. She introduced herself as Mary. The baby was Brandon.

"Nathan isn't home yet," she told the deputy. "He had a late meeting. Please have a seat. He should be here soon."

Doody took a seat on the couch. She seated herself in the rocking chair, and proceeded to rock her son. The room smelled like baby lotion and diaper cream. A handmade quilt covered much of the floor, held down in part by diapers, wipes, and soft toys. The baby had just been fed and bathed, and all was right with his world. Doody fervently hoped that it stayed that way.

"I need to ask you some questions about the night before your son was born," he began. "I'm the deputy who took your statement over the phone, but we need to re-check everyone's whereabouts that evening. What time did Mr. Taylor get home that night?"

She kissed the drowsy baby's cheek and answered, patting his back for a burp. "As I told you before, I think it was around ten-fifteen or ten-thirty. I remember watching part of the news before Nathan got home. I wanted to know how cold it was going to be the next day, so I'd know what to wear to the hospital."

"Which channel were you watching?" Doody wanted to be able to confirm the time.

"Channel six. I like their weather team. Cal Sisto said it was going to be cold and windy, with a good chance of rain, so I set out my raincoat and something warm to wear. Something I could still fit into." She smiled, and Doody squirmed.

"How did your husband seem after his meeting with Jack Hatfield?"

"He was very happy. Mr. Hatfield had given him a big order, and he'd taken the next few days off, so he could be with me at the hospital, and with our new son, of course." She shifted the baby carefully to her other shoulder and continued to rock.

"Do you know of any problems between Mr. Hatfield and your husband, Mrs. Taylor?"

"No, none whatsoever. Nathan told me about his father and Mr. Hatfield's mother, but he's been doing business with Mr. Hatfield for over a year without any problems. I think they both realized they weren't to blame."

She shook her head. "I just wish my mother-in-law could put it behind her."

"Put it behind her?"

"Well, she's never forgiven Nathan's father for getting himself killed like that. It turned her sour inside somehow. She didn't even want Nathan to get married, just wanted him to stay with her for the rest of his life."

The baby stretched, yawned, and went back to sleep without ever opening his eyes.

"Mrs. Taylor hates me. She hasn't even called or come by to see the baby. Can you imagine a grandmother not even wanting to see her new grandchild?"

Doody couldn't imagine it.

"She just sits and broods about the past; never seems to enjoy the present. I haven't seen her in months. Neither has Nathan because she's been so mean to me. We're not having any contact with her until she apologizes."

Doody was about to ask another question when the front door opened and Nathan Taylor walked in. He looked surprised to see the deputy in his living room, shook hands with him, then leaned over and kissed his wife's cheek and the sleeping baby's head.

"I saw your car out front, but I assumed it was someone visiting a neighbor. We don't get much company, just Mary's family," he finished lamely.

He sat down in a nearby chair while Doody explained that he had come by to recheck Taylor's whereabouts the night of the Hatfield murder.

"I'm sure I told the sheriff everything I could about that night. What else do you need to know?" He thrummed his fingers on the chair arm.

Doody checked his notes. There was something about this story that didn't fit. "Didn't you tell the sheriff that you got home a little after nine that night, Mr. Taylor?"

He thought for a minute. "Yes, that sounds about right."

Doody sighed. "According to your wife, it was actually a little after ten. The news was on."

There was a time gap of an hour or so in Taylor's alibi, and Doody had missed it before. Sheriff Dalton would be happy to hear about that.

"It couldn't have been that late. I did stop for gas, and I got my wife some Popsicles. Then I came straight home. You must be mistaken, honey." He turned to his wife.

Mary Taylor looked at her husband and then back toward Doody. "Yes, perhaps I was mistaken. I was very nervous that night, with the baby coming and all. I walked the floor a lot that evening. I must have been wrong about the time."

Great. Now she was lying, too. Doody had watched her closely when she answered. She'd looked over his left shoulder rather than at his face when she'd said she was mistaken about the time. People nearly always did that when they were about to tell a lie. And she'd been very certain about the news being on the television before Taylor came home. What reason could she have for lying except to protect her husband?

"Where did you get the gas and Popsicles?" He turned his attention back to the husband.

"The Quick Mart on the Loop. It's on my way home."

"I believe you told the sheriff that you didn't use your

credit card. Would anyone at the store remember you?" Doody asked.

"No," he responded. "It's a small station, but I doubt if they would remember me. It was very busy when I was there."

"Why didn't you use your credit card? Don't you need the receipts for your expense report?"

"They gave me a written receipt, but it doesn't have the time, just the date and how much I spent. My credit card is near the limit, so I haven't been using it. Sometimes the company is a little slow about reimbursing me, and my truck drinks gas like a hog at a water trough."

Taylor smiled and looked right at Doody, but Doody still didn't believe his story. He'd have to report this to Dalton. He'd found some important evidence in the case, even if it might be a bit late for the sheriff's taste. Maybe he should just shoot himself now and get it over with? Might be less painful.

"What about last night? Were you home all night long?" Doody asked.

Mary Taylor spoke before her husband. "Why last night? What does that have to do with Mr. Hatfield's death?" She frowned at the deputy.

"Someone else was killed on Market Street early this morning. We're trying to find out if the two cases are related," he answered.

"He was here all night long, from supper time on, about six o'clock. Isn't that right honey?" She looked at her husband. He nodded quickly in agreement.

"Anyone else verify that?" Doody asked.

They looked at each other and shook their heads.

Doody stood up to leave. "I need to see your truck again, Mr. Taylor. The sheriff wants to make sure there's still nothing missing. Mind if I take care of that now?"

"I was attending a seminar all day, so I drove my car. My truck is locked up at the warehouse. I'll be in Metropolis tomorrow. I could bring it by your office then, if that would be soon enough."

"I suppose so. You can talk to the sheriff then. And bring your inventory list along."

"Sure, I keep it on my laptop. I'll come by first thing in the morning." Taylor stood up and saw Doody to the door.

Doody headed down the Loop to the station Taylor had mentioned. He got gas, then went inside and got a Coke and a bag of peanuts. While he poured the peanuts into the Coke and waited for the fizz to stop, he questioned the evening attendant.

"Yeah, I worked that night," the attendant responded. "But we get a lot of business every night. No way I can remember if your guy was here."

"Could we check your videotapes from the security camera to see if our man came in and what time that might have been?" Doody asked between sips. Nothing beat the taste of salty peanuts in a fizzing Coke.

"Could if we had any," was the answer. "Camera's been out over a month now and the boss is too tightfisted to fix it. He figures just the sight of the camera will scare the thieves off." The clerk rolled his eyes.

Doody went back to his car and headed home thinking about what he would tell Dalton at the next meeting. Taylor's alibi was very thin for both murders. No credit card slip and no video to back him up for the time of Hatfield's murder.

Taylor could've had a grudge against Jack Hatfield because of his parents, in spite of his denial to the sheriff. And he could've killed Big Ed out of fear that he'd seen something. The local papers had mentioned Simmons spotting the body.

Taylor had probably spent enough time in Metropolis to know about Market Street being deserted at night, but wouldn't have known about Simmons's habit of sleeping in the stairwell at Mrs. Lipinski's. Taylor had the strength to have killed Hatfield and hung his body on the statue as well as bash in Big Ed's skull with a hammer. He was looking better and better as a suspect, and Doody was feeling worse and worse.

He swallowed the last of the Coke and peanuts and wiped his hand on his pants.

CHAPTER 29

"Did you stop by Deb's on the way home like you promised?"

Dalton rubbed his eyes. "No, honey, I didn't. I'm sorry, I forgot. I was busy all day, and I just came straight home as soon as I could. I will, soon, I promise."

He paused in the midst of hanging his jacket in the closet. "Is it something urgent? Is something wrong with Debby or Chuck? Should I go over there right now?"

"No, of course not. I would've told you if something was wrong." She headed toward the kitchen. "She just wants to see you, that's all. She has something she wants to talk over with you, daughter to father. Go by there as soon as you can, okay?"

"I promise, first chance I get I'll go over there," he said as he eased himself slowly into his usual chair. "What's that great smell?"

"Chicken potpie and salad. I can't seem to feed you fat-free, so I'm now aiming for healthier." She placed a plate in front of him.

"Any leads on Big Ed yet? Do you think his murder is tied to Jack's?" She poured him a big glass of iced tea.

"No leads, but I do think the murders are connected. Big Ed either saw something the night Jack died, or the killer thought he did and decided to keep him quiet." He took a sip of tea. "Worst-case scenario, someone could be targeting anyone alone on Market Street at night. That possibility worries me the most."

"That is a scary thought. I just can't imagine that happening in a small town like Metropolis." She sat down across from him. "I did some research on Big Ed today for the feature column. Such a waste. Everyone says he was a brilliant lawyer, but no one seems to know what drove him to scuttle his career like that. Did you find any family that would claim him?"

"Yeah. His landlady had an address for his ex-wife. George contacted her this afternoon. She's coming down from Chicago tomorrow to make the arrangements." He reached for a napkin. "She'll probably have him buried here."

The first bite of potpie burned his tongue, and he took another quick gulp of tea.

"Well, I hope you catch the killer. No one in this town will rest easy until you do. What about the abandoned baby? Any leads on his parents?"

"Not yet. Unless we get a break, it's going to be really tough to tie that baby to his parents. So far none of the hospitals or doctors in the area have treated any patients who might have given birth without medical assistance. In short, we don't have a clue as to who the mother or the father might be."

"But Jack's case is the one that's really bothering you, isn't it? Or is it just so many in such a short time?"

He took another bite, found it had cooled enough, and continued chewing.

"I guess it's all three. Big Ed was a harmless drunk. He never hurt anyone, 'cept maybe himself. The baby didn't have to die like that. The mother had other choices. And Jack, well, I guess I do feel guilty about him." He paused for another sip of tea.

"I hadn't seen much of him for a long time, just to say 'Hi, how are you?' whenever we met on the street. Ruby said something had been bothering him for several months, but he wouldn't tell her what it was. Peggy and Mark don't seem to know what it was either."

"If he wouldn't tell them, it isn't likely he'd have told you, is it? Jack was pretty private."

"I know. I just keep thinking I should've stayed more in touch over the years. It must've been tough on him taking care of the business and Peggy and Mark." He wiped his mouth with the napkin.

"He doesn't seem to have had any close friends, except Ruby, and I gather they weren't that close lately either. She said he'd begun breaking dates with her."

"That's odd. They always seemed so comfortable with each other. Wonder what went wrong."

"Ruby didn't seem to know. I keep wondering why I didn't find the time to walk down to the store more often, visit with Jack, and see how things were going. How did I let myself get so busy that I didn't have time for an old friend?"

"People do drift apart, honey, without meaning to. It just happens. This last year has been a tough one on our family, with Debby losing the baby and Dan being so far away." She reached across the table and touched his hand. "It was much easier when they lived at home and we could keep an eye on them. Anyhow, you shouldn't blame yourself for this."

"I suppose so. I just can't seem to get past this feeling of guilt, like I should've done more. Everyone we've talked to says he was different, and I hadn't even noticed. If Jack was in trouble, I should have seen it."

"You can't do any more for Jack. It's too late for that. But we could both do something for his brother and sister. That might help you feel better."

"Like what?" He reached for a second helping of potpie.

"Well, for starters, I could go over tomorrow and pick up my dishes. That would give me an excuse to check on them. I could

171

even take some of this huge potpie I baked. We haven't even eaten half of it." She poured him some more tea. "I was thinking about calling the minister who spoke at Jack's funeral. Maybe he'd have some ideas about helping them."

"I don't know what else to do. I've got Peters and Edwards going over there tonight to question them again. But I'd really appreciate it if you would check on them, too. I'll be busy going over the deputies' reports tomorrow. At least with three of them, I will. I had to suspend Billy Wilson today."

"Suspend him? He's your best deputy."

He repeated the story Wilson had told him about his marriage to Barb, and his affair with Ruby. Dalton was comfortable sharing the story with Ginger; she would never repeat anything sensitive that he told her, and he liked to get her feedback.

"I'm stunned," she said when he finished. "Barb is so together, so efficient, so elegant." She shook her head. "I can't imagine her creating a cold, dead marriage like that and expecting Billy to go along with it. It's a wonder he lasted this long."

"I felt sorry for him, too, but that doesn't alter the fact that he lied to me and turned in a false statement. I suppose the affair explains why Ruby kept her distance from Jack's family at the funeral home. Guilty conscience." Dalton pushed his empty plate away and leaned back in his chair.

"Wilson is going to have to get his life in order before I let him come back off suspension."

"Which means you're operating short-handed."

"Yeah, but no help for it."

The phone rang during the clean-up operation. Dalton answered it. It was his youngest, Dan, asking to bring a friend home for the upcoming holidays.

"Of course, son, your friends are always welcome here. Who is it?" As Dalton listened to the response, Ginger's eyebrows went up, but she held her peace.

"Fine. Paula can sleep in Deb's old room. I'm sure your mom won't mind giving up her sewing room for a few days." Dalton glanced sheepishly at his wife.

"Need any money for the trip home?"

Upon receiving a negative response, Dalton launched into a discussion of their favorite football team and how the season was going, ignoring his wife's impatient foot taping.

When the conversation finally ran down, Dalton reluctantly passed the phone to his wife so she could begin to grill their son about the new female in his life. Dan's eagerness to introduce his friend to the whole family reminded Dalton again that he hadn't kept his promise to stop by and see his daughter. He made up his mind to take care of it as soon as possible.

CHAPTER 30

The next morning Dalton woke up a good hour before the alarm went off. He hadn't slept well and couldn't get back to sleep now. He rolled out of bed and went to the bathroom to shower, not worried about being quiet for his sleeping wife.

Her zombie-like morning behavior had always baffled him, and she had passed the trait on to their son. Thankfully Deb was just like her dad, an early riser who jumped out of bed and started the day by singing in the shower. It was beyond him why anyone would have to sit and stare and drink coffee before they could successfully communicate with other human beings.

While Dalton showered, he thought about his daughter's reasons for wanting him to come by and see her. She rarely asked him to do that. She usually came by to see them.

She'd be up by the time he was dressed. He could run by there for coffee on his way to work. Satisfied with his decision, he toweled off with one of the extra-large towels his wife kept in the linen closet for him and began to shave. He hummed off-key as he ran the electric razor over his chin.

Twenty minutes later he kissed his sleeping wife goodbye, headed out the door to his car, and drove over to the highway where the local donut shop was located. The donuts at South Paw's were homemade and the couple of dozen he picked up were still warm. He set them carefully on the seat next to him and headed back toward town to Debby's house.

Debby greeted him with a bear hug as forceful as her mother's. "Dad, you shouldn't have brought donuts. You know I can't resist them."

"Neither can my deputies and the way the investigations are going, they need a sugar high."

They sat at the kitchen table and watched the early morning activity at the bird feeder. A hungry squirrel hung by one leg from a nearby limb, stretching his arm as far as he could, trying to reach around the baffle that Chuck had put up to keep him away. When that plan failed, the squirrel backed up the limb and took a running leap at the feeder, only to hit the baffle and land on the ground with a splat. He shook himself off, climbed back up the tree to a low limb, and stretched out as if to rest and plan his next form of attack. Father and daughter laughed as each reached for another donut.

Dalton doctored his coffee and brought up the subject at hand.

"Your mom said you wanted to talk to me. I should've gotten by here sooner, but these cases have kept me pretty busy, and by the end of the day I've been too tired to think. I'm really sorry, honey. What did you want to talk to me about?"

"I have some good news. Now don't start acting like a worried father here." She grinned at her dad. "Chuck and I are expecting again."

He put his cup down with a bang. "Already? But it hasn't been that long since, well, since the other…" he trailed off lamely.

"I've already seen Dr. Lewis, and he says everything looks fine so far, Dad. No reason why this one shouldn't be perfectly healthy. He plans to keep a close eye on me and do periodic ultrasounds to check on the baby. I wanted break the news to you myself, so you wouldn't worry."

"I see you're already practicing rocking." Who else had he seen doing that recently?

"I got into the habit when Trisha was born. After we lost her I caught myself doing it unconsciously. Lots of mothers who lose babies do it. At least that's what they said at the support group Chuck and I joined."

"I want you to promise me you will take really good care of yourself. No lifting or hard work. If something needs to be done and Chuck is gone, call me, and I'll run by no matter how busy I am at work."

He really wanted grandchildren, but more than that, he wanted his little girl to be safe and well. He didn't want to see her suffer again like she had last year.

"I promise to be very careful, Dad, and Chuck has already given me the same lecture—several times over."

She grinned at him again. Her freckled nose crinkled up in a way that reminded him of her mother. Ginger had been pretty fearless about having and raising children too.

"This one is going to be fine. I just know it."

The brave words didn't fool him. But it was getting late and it was time for him to go to work. He kissed his daughter's cheek, made her promise again to be careful, and headed to his car.

(HAPTER 31

When he arrived at the detention center a few minutes later, Dalton didn't have to bother calling a meeting. The deputies were waiting in his office, ready to share what they had learned the evening before. The smell of the fresh donuts Dalton placed next to the coffee maker was an added incentive.

Doody Jenson started off the meeting. He told Dalton about his conversation with Taylor's wife and the lie she'd told.

"Maybe Taylor's mother taught him to hate Hatfield's family as much as she did and to want revenge," Doody said as he launched into his theory. "If Taylor wasn't ready to put the past behind him, he could've taken this job just to get to know Hatfield, get him to trust him, catch him off guard. He has no real alibi for either murder, so he could've committed both. He promised to come in first thing this morning with his laptop and show you his inventory, so you can question him for yourself."

Doody reached for a second donut as he wound up his report. "Sure hate to think that it's Taylor. He has a nice wife and a beautiful little boy. Shame Baby Doe didn't have her for a mother."

Doody leaned back in his chair and concentrated on the donut. Peters picked up her coffee for a quick sip and told the group about her visit to Miss Mamie's with Edwards.

"Even I couldn't tell Mark and Peggy apart from that distance, except by their clothes and where they sat, and my eyes are much better than hers. I wondered if maybe Mark killed his brother for some reason we haven't hit on, and his sister covered for him by wearing his clothes and sitting on the couch while he disposed of the body."

Peters set down her donut and coffee so she could talk with her hands.

"What I can't figure out is why Mark would have killed his brother. Miss Mamie was wrong about Peggy's size too, but she said Peggy's lost quite a bit of weight lately."

Peters looked down at her ample frame.

"Wish I knew her secret. I've tried every diet known to woman: high fiber, low carb, no meat, no fat, no fun. The only time I ever lost that much weight in such a short time was right after giving birth."

For a few seconds the deputies all stared at each other. Then they all tried to talk at once. Dalton held up his hand for quiet.

"Okay, hold on, everyone. It's true we have no leads on a mother for Baby Doe. Now we find out that Peggy has lost considerable weight recently."

As he spoke, the memory of how Peggy had sat on the couch and rocked while he told her about her brother's death came back to him.

"My daughter Debby is expecting again. She gave me the good news this morning. While we were talking, Deb kept rocking back and forth the same way Peggy did the morning I told her about Jack's death."

Dalton paused for a second and rubbed his hand on his chin while he thought. "I thought at the time it was because Peggy was in shock, but Deb says many mothers do that when they've lost a baby. Peggy hasn't been well since Jack's death. I put it down to grief, but it could also be from that afterbirth bit Jeffords was talking about."

Edwards spoke up. "If Hatfield found out his sister was pregnant, that could be what was bothering him all these months."

"True," Dalton said. "But what puzzles me is the fact that Peggy rarely goes out or mingles with people. How did she manage to get close enough to any guy to get pregnant?"

The deputies chewed on donuts and theories for several seconds. Edwards broke the silence. "Nathan Taylor has been selling to the hardware store for over a year. Jack wouldn't have been home twenty-four hours a day, and Taylor called at the store real regular."

"True," Peters agreed. "Taylor says he met Peggy Hatfield only once, and she says she doesn't remember him at all, but it's possible they know each other very well and have kept that a secret. After all, Taylor is married."

Doody Jenson interrupted. "Yeah, and Baby Doe had light, wavy hair. So does Taylor. But the whole scenario doesn't make sense. Hatfield must've been upset about his sister being pregnant."

Doody stopped as if mulling things over. "If he knew it was Taylor's baby, why would Hatfield have agreed to meet him at the restaurant that night, and why be so friendly? The waitress said they both seemed to be enjoying themselves. A man like Hatfield wouldn't continue to do business with someone who got his sister pregnant and then didn't own up to it."

"Obviously Hatfield knew his sister was pregnant, but suppose she refused to tell him who the father was?" Peters dusted powdered sugar off her pants. "If she rarely went out, she could've skipped seeing a doctor as well. She has the baby, possibly with the help of brother Mark. Miss Mamie said he rarely goes out, but we know Jack often went out on business or to be with Ruby Miller."

Peters' detecting wheels were in full forward motion. "Suppose Hatfield is out, and the baby comes. Mark is none too bright, so he maybe doesn't know how to deliver a baby or take care of it after it's born. They let it bleed to death, either accidentally or on purpose. Not knowing what else to do, he buries it on the Windhorst farm, not realizing we're in for a heavy rain that will wash the grave out."

Her thoughts struck Dalton as being right on target.

"Jack Hatfield is horrified, but what can he do? The baby's dead and buried, so he thinks. No way to find the father that started this whole mess."

Dalton watched as she reached for another napkin. No doubt about it. Peters was every bit as sharp as Wilson.

The rest of Peters's theory revolved around the two men meeting at the restaurant. Peters was certain that Hatfield had somehow figured out Taylor was the father of his sister's baby, and that he'd have wanted to take some sort of action against Taylor.

"Or, maybe it wasn't Mark who buried the baby," Peters said. "If Peggy or Taylor had let that baby die, and Hatfield found out, Taylor could have killed him to keep him quiet. We only have Taylor's word that he left Hatfield in the parking lot of the restaurant. They could have gone somewhere to talk privately, and Taylor, threatened with exposure and the likelihood of losing his job and family, might have become desperate enough to kill Hatfield."

She reached for the coffee pot to refill her cup, and then offered warm-ups to the others.

Edwards dropped in his thoughts. "So maybe Taylor somehow distracts Hatfield, strangles him from behind, cuts off his head with a tool from his truck in an attempt to hide the true cause of death, puts him on the statue, and goes home to his wife like nothing ever happened."

"Yep. I bet he even keeps a tarp in that truck that would've kept the blood off his clothes. And I bet right now it's at the bottom of the Ohio River. Make any sense? Peters looked around the room for confirmation of her theory. The deputies nodded.

"Before we get too excited here, let's get some solid evidence on this," Dalton answered. But he'd bet she wasn't far off the mark with her ideas.

"Edwards, call the coroner. Ask him to contact the state's attorney's office and get a court order for the Taylor baby's birth records along with a blood sample, and ask Jeffords to pick them up. Taylor said his son was born at Lourdes Hospital in Paducah. Doody, you find Taylor and make sure he does get in here for another little talk."

Dalton turned to the other deputies. "Peters, call Evansville and see if the DNA report on Baby Doe is ready. We'll have Jeffords transport the Taylor baby's blood sample to the forensic pathologist in Evansville for comparison. When we have some solid evidence, I'll confront Peggy. With any luck, she'll tell us everything we need to know."

The deputies swallowed donuts, wiped mouths, and headed for the door. As they went out, Billy Wilson came in, and Doody gave him a high five. Dalton indicated the visitor's chair, and Wilson sat down after closing the door.

"Barb and I have talked. She finally calmed down and she's willing to get some counseling. I guess it took me moving out and taking the kids to make her realize I was serious."

"I hope it works, Billy. I'd like to see you keep your family together," Dalton said.

"So would I, but the odds are way against us."

Wilson leaned forward and put his elbows on his knees.

"Barb has finally opened up and told me something she's been keeping secret all these years. She was sexually abused by her uncle—her mom's younger brother—from the time she was a little girl until he died when she was about eleven."

"Her family didn't know?"

"Her folks don't have a clue and they let him baby-sit her all the time. He said if she told anyone they would think she was to

181

blame and punish her. Barb believed him, until she got older. By then she was too ashamed to tell."

Dalton thought of his own daughter. He'd have killed anyone who tried that with Deb, without even a pang of conscience.

"Barb's mom idolized her younger brother, and Barb didn't think she'd believe her. Even now she's afraid to tell. She's kept this bottled up so long and let our marriage go so sour that I don't know if we can save anything, but for the girls' sakes I have to try."

Dalton nodded. Too bad that even a town this small wasn't immune to that kind of sickness.

"The abuse made Barb angry, and she turned that anger on me. I guess it does that to a woman. I suppose it's hard for us guys to understand that sort of thing, but Barb said it killed something inside her."

"What about Ruby?"

"I called her and told her it's over. I can't see her anymore. She took it pretty hard, and I feel real bad about that. I'm going to miss her, but I have to try to save my marriage. Truth is, I still love Barb, in spite of everything."

Wilson cleared his throat.

"I'd rather no one else knew about this. So would Barb. Can we keep this between us?"

"Of course. Good luck with the counseling. Let me know how it goes," Dalton said.

Wilson stood up and looked at Dalton. "Will I be able to get my job back?"

"Yes. I don't want to lose a good deputy like you. Just don't ever let anything like this happen again." Dalton stood. "I want you to take the rest of the week off to think things over and work on getting your life straight. Hopefully by then the case will be solved. We got a couple of breaks this morning, so we'll see. Check in with me Monday, okay?"

Wilson shook Dalton's hand and left.

George Means leaned in Dalton's office door as Wilson walked out, armed with a screwdriver and wrench in one hand, a can of WD 40 and part of the front door in the other.

"Wife just called; said she's going to the Hatfields' apartment to deliver some food. When she's done visiting, she'll come by and pick you up for a late lunch if you're free. Said to tell you it's a celebration, on account of her test coming back negative."

Means frowned at Dalton, "Uh, which test was that, Sheriff?" he asked.

Dalton smiled. "Just routine, George, nothing for you to worry about." Nothing for him to worry about either. Ginger's breast biopsy was negative. What a relief. The tightness in his chest eased considerably for the first time in days.

A late lunch sounded fine to Dalton. He was still full of the donuts he'd eaten with his daughter and his deputies.

"Call Ginger back and tell her I'll be waiting. I want to go over these reports again, in case I missed anything. What are you doing with that screwdriver and those parts?"

"Fixin' the front door. Every time it bangs shut it scares me right out of my seat. Sometimes a man has to take matters into his own hands, but if your deputies keep running out of here like the building's on fire it's going to be tough to get the job done by the end of my shift."

He turned to leave the doorway, and then turned back.

"So, you really think that Taylor fella and Peggy Hatfield had something going on, Sheriff?"

Means had obviously been listening in again. Thankfully, Wilson had made sure the door was shut before discussing his private life.

"I won't know anything for certain till the tests are all in, George. I'll let you know when I know. Maybe you'd better get back to work on the door before anyone else comes in. And don't forget to call Ginger."

"I won't forget," he grumbled. "Guess my memory is as good as anybody else's around here."

He shuffled a few feet toward his desk, and then turned back to the doorway of Dalton's office.

"Oh, forgot to tell you something. While you were meeting with Wilson, Nathan Taylor called. He'll be by sometime after lunch with the inventory you wanted to see. He's running late on account of being up most of the night with the new baby. Said he had an important meeting before coming in."

Means took another step toward his desk, and then turned around again.

"Also said he wants to make a change in his statement about the night Jack Hatfield died. Something about stopping by his mother's house on the way home and not wanting his wife to know." Means shook his head. "Seems those two don't get along none too well, and he's really scared of his wife finding out that he sees his mother regularly. Said his mother could verify where he was after he left Hatfield and before he got home. I told him he'd have to discuss that with you."

"Thanks, George."

How convenient. Taylor had another alibi, just when he needed one. Dalton gathered up the rest of the donuts, put them in a plastic container, burped the lid, and placed them near the coffee pot. He'd have to try not to eat them all before the deputies returned. He went back to his desk and began straightening papers and reading reports.

If Taylor really had stopped by his mother's that night, then he would still be covered for the time of Jack's death. But could they believe Mrs. Taylor in view of her daughter-in-law's statement that she'd never gotten over the death of her husband? Could that "important meeting" Taylor had this morning be with his own mother to make sure their stories matched?

184

Dalton sighed. This case had more twists and turns than the Ohio River bed and he was having a tough time trying to straighten them all out. He would reserve judgment on Taylor's new alibi until the results of the blood tests came in on the two babies. If their DNA matched, Mr. Taylor would have some serious explaining to do. Dalton wasn't about to let him get away with murder.

(HAPT€R 32

The pile of paperwork on Dalton's left buzzed. He dug under it and pressed a button.

"Yes, George?"

"Miz Ruby Miller is here to see you about the Hatfield case. She says it's important."

"Show her to my office, please, George."

Dalton made a quick stab at straightening his desk, and gave up when the effort only made the mess worse.

The elderly dispatcher gestured Ruby into a chair and began to hover over her.

"Can I get you anything, ma'am? I make a mean cup of coffee."

You got that right, Dalton thought.

"Thank you, George, I'll take care of Ms. Miller. You go back to work and don't worry about us."

Means huffed out the door.

Ruby pulled off her jacket and smoothed it across her lap. She pulled a tissue out of her pocket and mopped her swollen eyes. Whatever she wanted, it wasn't good.

Dalton prayed she wasn't going to ask him to talk to Wilson on her behalf, now that Wilson had, somewhat belatedly, decided to give his marriage another try. If that was it, she was doomed to disappointment. Instead, her first words surprised him.

"Sheriff, I still haven't told you everything I know about Jack."
She sniffed and wiped her eyes again. This was going to take a while. Dalton leaned back in his chair and tried to make sympathetic noises.

"Just take your time, Ruby. I'm in no hurry. Would you care for some coffee?"

She nodded, and he got up to fix them each a cup. He was glad to have an excuse to turn away. Women crying always brought out his soft side, and right now he didn't figure he could afford to be soft. What more could she possibly have to tell him?

"I know how fond you were of Jack. This whole town thought he walked on water. So did I, for that matter. At least until lately."

Dalton handed her a cup of coffee and sat down, forgetting his own. The alarm bells he heard when he found his old friend's body were clanging loudly inside his head again.

"What happened to make you change your mind?" He hoped his tone sounded neutral.

"Jack was always a perfect gentleman. Maybe a little too perfect. Sometimes he seemed, oh, I don't know, a little detached from our relationship." She looked up from her cup.

"It seemed like he was standing back, watching us both from a distance. Like nothing could touch him inside, where he really lived. We were close physically, but not emotionally. Does that make any sense?"

Doesn't make much sense at all, Dalton thought, nodding as if he understood perfectly.

Ruby continued, explaining to Dalton that her first husband had been a control freak, wanting to know her every move. She'd liked the fact that Jack gave her plenty of space and made few demands. She'd always assumed that the deaths of his parents had prevented Jack from getting too close, and the relationship that had developed between them had seemed normal at the time.

She frowned as if choosing her words carefully. Dalton could see why his deputy had found Ruby appealing. She sipped her coffee before continuing.

"You asked me if I thought anything had been bothering Jack lately. I told you yes, but that I didn't know what it was. That was true, and I still don't know. What I didn't tell you was that Jack had changed a great deal in his treatment of me."

In what way?" Dalton wasn't sure he wanted to hear the answer to his question.

"He began to abuse me. At first it was just emotional, telling me I wasn't very smart, treating me in a disrespectful way, things like that."

The skin on the back of Dalton's neck began to crawl. He'd heard similar stories before, but not about someone he admired.

"What did you do about it?"

"I really did think the business might be failing, or there might be something worrying him that I didn't know about. I tried talking to him about it, tried to find out what was wrong, but he'd only get really angry and shout at me to shut up."

Dalton got up and walked back to the coffee pot. He really didn't want any but he had to move around. He returned to his desk and set the full cup on a pile of papers, making a telltale ring on the top report.

"Did you think about getting help, or calling off the relationship?"

"I told him I didn't think we should see each other any more. That was the first time he got physical with me. He shook me really hard."

Dalton's chair came forward with a squawk.

"Did you tell anyone? File a report with us?"

"No. Jack apologized a lot and promised it would never happen again. I believed him. The next day he sent a dozen long stemmed red roses. We'd been together for years and he'd never done anything like that, so of course I thought he was sincere."

Ruby broke down and sobbed into the worn tissue for several minutes. Dalton scrounged for a fresh box on the cabinet behind him and handed it to her.

"What happened after that? Did he keep his promise?"

Dalton figured he already knew what her answer would be, but he wanted to hear it from her.

"No, he got worse. Whenever I did anything to upset him, he would grab me and hit me. He was smart, Sheriff; he always hit where it wouldn't show, my back, stomach, or hips. He began to get rough with sex as well. Really rough."

"Why didn't you call our office and file a complaint after he left you to go to work. We would have protected you."

"Would you have? How could I know that for sure? You were one of his best friends. You might have covered for him."

Dalton shook his head. He felt sick. Jack may have been his friend, but protecting the citizens of Massac County was the sheriff's primary job, and he would not have allowed any friendship to come before doing that job. Somehow he had failed to communicate that to at least one of his fellow citizens.

"Jack said that if I told anyone, no one in this town would believe me. They'd think I was crazy because we'd been together for so long and there had never been a whisper of a problem."

She was probably right about that.

"He said he'd tell people that he'd been trying to break it off and that accusing him was my way of getting even. He said he would swear he'd never touched me and that I'd probably hurt myself to make those bruises. It would have been my word against his. Who do you think people would have believed? Who would you have believed?"

Dalton felt himself grow cold. He wasn't sure he knew the answers to her questions.

"In all honesty, Ruby, I can't say which one of you I would have believed. But I assure you there would have been a thorough investigation, and I would have taken steps to make certain that you were safe. I just wish you had come to me sooner."

She nodded and wiped her nose. "I know, I was a coward. I should have done something about this while Jack was still alive. At least I did have sense enough to call for help the night I heard the prowler. I was afraid it was Jack checking on me, or maybe even planning on hurting me worse."

She swallowed another sip of coffee and told Dalton about how her affair with his deputy had begun that night. It wasn't a story he was eager to hear, but he let her talk.

"I have never been so relieved to see anyone in my life. I needed Billy so much that night. From then on, he would come by to check on me when he knew Jack wouldn't be there. We met in the park reserve a few times as well. I knew Jack never went there."

Maybe Jack didn't, but they should have realized other people did. It was a wonder no one had caught them.

"The truth is, I was using Billy. I thought if I could get close to him, maybe I could prove Jack was beating me. Then I would've at least had someone on my side. But it backfired on me. I love Billy more than I thought possible, and now I've lost him, too."

Dalton was surprised at her confession, but he wasn't going to judge her for what she'd done. He figured she and Billy had both paid a high enough price already. He passed her the small wastebasket under his desk so she could dump the wet tissues.

"Why didn't you tell me about this when I came to your house? Jack was dead. He couldn't have hurt you any more?"

"Because I still didn't think you would believe me. And I didn't want Billy to find out about any of it. I was too ashamed. Now that he's broken it off to go back to his wife, I don't care what happens to me." She leaned forward. "I thought about it long and hard, and I realized that the truth might matter. It could have some bearing on Jack's death. I hope you believe me. I don't have any proof. The bruises have all faded."

No proof indeed. With the bruises gone, and no complaint filed, it was her word against that of a dead man who was admired and respected by everyone who knew him.

Means buzzed Dalton again. "Yes, George?"

"Thought you'd want to know, the state's attorney's office just called. She gave the coroner the court order he needed, but she wants you in her office this afternoon with a full report on how all this ties together. Secretary wanted to speak to you, but I told her you were interviewing a witness."

"Thanks, George, I owe you one. Ask Deputy Peters to step into my office. I have a job for her."

Dalton turned back to Ruby.

"Even though Jack is dead, I'm still going to look into this. It could be important to the case. I need to get a formal statement from you and have you sign it. Are you willing to do that?"

"Of course. I'd just as soon get it over with now if I could."

She placed her cup on the one paperless spot on Dalton's desk as Peters tapped on the office door.

"I appreciate your coming in, Ruby. I know it took a lot of courage. I'll let you know what we find out."

She nodded and Dalton turned to Peters. "Ms. Miller has a statement to give. I'd like you to take care of that for me."

"Sure, boss." Peters ushered Ruby out of Dalton's office.

Dalton returned to his desk to mull over what he'd just heard. He wasn't a violent man, and throughout his career prisoners had more often than not been subdued by his size and the look in his eye, rather than any physical pressure on his part.

He couldn't fathom the need some men had to threaten or hit someone weaker than themselves.

Jack had never seemed to be that type of man. Could Dalton have been so mistaken in his friend? Or did Ruby perhaps have some hidden agenda that he wasn't aware of yet? Whatever the answer, he was determined to do his best to find it.

If Jack was an abuser, Dalton wanted to know; and if he wasn't, Dalton would clear his old friend's name. He reached for the forensic pathologist's preliminary reports and spent some time trying to concentrate on them.

He was still studying the reports when Means stuck his head back inside the door.

"Don't want to alarm you none, Sheriff, but we just got a nine-one-one call from the Hatfields' apartment. Woman didn't give her name, just said she needed an ambulance there right away and to tell you to come too. Then she dropped the phone. I can still hear voices, but I can't raise anybody."

Ginger's supposed to be at the Hatfields' by now, Dalton thought. He jumped up and headed around his desk toward the still-open front door that Means had not yet managed to conquer.

CHAPTER 33

Dalton bolted through the detention center door, nearly knocking over the ladder Means had been using and raced to the corner of the Super Museum. Rounding the corner, he collided with a small group of foreign tourists peeking in the window. He apologized over his shoulder and shot between two parked cars, into the street.

Dalton narrowly managed to avoid being run over by a tour bus before hitting the sidewalk on the opposite side of the street at a full sprint. He hadn't moved this fast since he'd chased an escapee from Menard Prison through a cornfield near Joppa. He was discovering that sidewalks were much easier to run on than cornfields with dried stubs.

Dalton was halfway to the Hatfields' apartment when it dawned on him that his car would have been much quicker. He turned the corner at Seventh and headed toward the metal stairway. He put out a new burst of speed when he saw his wife's car parked near the back of the Hatfields' store. What if something had happened to her?

He clanged up the stairs two at a time and began pounding on the door. He peered through the glass, impatient to see someone coming to answer. Instead, he saw a woman's legs stretched across the floor behind the kitchen table. They were much too thick to be Ginger's, he'd know her legs anywhere; these must be Peggy's.

He leaned back, hunched over, and prepared to throw his ample weight against the old door. A split-second before his shoulder hit wood, Ginger appeared in the window, her hand reaching for the lock to let him in.

Dalton was so glad to see his wife unhurt that all he could do was grab and hug her. She pushed him away impatiently and pointed to the floor.

"I called nine-one-one." Her voice was shaky. "The ambulance should be here any minute."

Dalton's glance followed to where Ginger pointed. Peggy Hatfield lay on the kitchen floor, her face a pale, bluish color. She was breathing heavily, and blood leaked out from under her dress and across the floor. Ginger had placed a pillow under her head and covered her with a blanket, but Peggy had pushed it away.

Dalton went around the table, bent over Peggy, and felt her pulse. Her skin was clammy to the touch, and her forehead and upper lip were beaded with sweat. She was going into shock. He ordered Ginger to help him place a kitchen chair under Peggy's feet to elevate her legs. An awful smell surrounded her, like fish or raw liver. She'd been sick nearby.

"When I got here, she let me in. I could see how weak she was, and I realized the smell was coming from her, not the trash," Ginger began. "She must have a horrible infection. I tried to get her to go lie down, but she refused. We started for the living room, and she collapsed. I tried to make her comfortable. I didn't know what else to do."

Dalton squeezed his wife's shoulder. He knew she was about to cry. Peggy was conscious, but very ill. She tried to speak, failed, and then tried again.

"I'm glad you're both here. I need to talk to someone before it's too late. Please look after Mark. He'll need your help."

"Why don't you just rest until the ambulance arrives, Peggy, and we get you to the hospital?" Dalton suggested.

With a determined effort, she said, "No, I have to tell you now. I know how sick I am. Childbed fever, isn't that what they used to call it? My grandmother died of it. She had a change-of-life pregnancy. Her baby died, too."

She choked out something between a cough and a chuckle. "Funny. I didn't think people died of it these days, did you?"

Dalton shook his head.

She turned to look at Ginger. "I read your column in the paper. You're not like that man who usually writes the stories about other people's troubles. You really care. I want you to write my story, please?"

When Ginger nodded, Peggy turned back toward Dalton. "Don't blame Mark. None of this was his fault. It was all mine. I killed Jack. I killed Big Ed Simmons, too."

Dalton was stunned.

"Mark wasn't involved. You have to believe that. He only took Jack's body away for me. I told him to tie something heavy on it and drop it into the river along with the other things. You never would have found Jack that way."

Dalton's jaw dropped. He looked across at Ginger. Her eyes were huge.

"Why, Peggy?" Ginger wanted to know. "Jack was the one who took care of you and Mark all these years. If it hadn't been for him, you two would've wound up in an orphanage or a foster home."

"That would have been heaven compared to life in this home."

Dalton didn't understand. "I know Jack was a little over-protective of you. But why kill him? Was it because he came between you and the baby's father? We know Baby Doe was yours and that Nathan Taylor was the father. I was just waiting for the test results before confronting either of you."

Peggy gave a short bark of a laugh, and then grimaced

when the effort caused pain.

"Jack was the father of my baby, Joe. Like your home-town hero now? I'll spare you the details as much as possible. Don't think I have much time left anyways."

She told her story in short sentences with pauses for breaths between each effort. Her story wasn't a pretty one.

"Jack was Mother's pet. She never had time for Mark or me. Just for Jack. And he was very jealous of her. Didn't want to share her with anyone. Especially not another man."

Meaning Nathan Taylor's father?

"Jack has been beating and raping me ever since our parents died. He felt guilty, and he took it out on me. Said if I told anyone, he'd kill me. He meant it!"

"But why? What happened to your parents wasn't your fault, or his," Dalton said.

"Oh, but it was. He caused their deaths. Told Daddy about Mother's affair. He didn't think Daddy would kill her, just stop her. Afterward, Jack couldn't face what he'd done."

Dalton was too shocked to speak. So, Ruby had been tell-ing the truth about the abuse.

"Jack said that without us around, Mark would be alone. Mark couldn't survive that. No family, no one to turn to. Jack rarely let me out. Told people I was a hermit. I don't even know Mr. Taylor. Jack never let me get to know any other men."

Peggy smiled grimly at the look on Dalton's face.

"I let myself get fat over the years, hoping he'd leave me alone. It didn't work. When I realized I was pregnant, it was easy to hide the news from my brothers for several months. I thought the baby might bring out the truth, help me find a way of escape."

Dalton tried to imagine what her life had been like and failed. He'd never had to live in constant fear.

"When he found out about it, Jack was furious. Beat me

196

to make me lose it. Guess I was tougher than he thought." She looked as if she was proud of that fact.

"Told Jack I'd had enough. I was going to tell someone, anyone, what he'd done to me. He promised he'd never touch me again if I kept quiet." She shook her head again.

"Should've known he was lying." She shivered, and Ginger tucked the blanket back around her.

"Jack said he'd deliver the baby here. No one would know. Said he'd leave the baby somewhere safe. If nobody knew where it came from, it might have a chance of finding a good home. I really thought he meant it." A tear trickled down her cheek as she spoke.

"Jack put me in the bathtub when the pains started. He said he'd read in a book…that it was easier on the mother…to be in warm water. Then he sent Mark to Paducah…to get some things for the birth."

Dalton noticed that she was speaking in small bursts as she hurried to finish her story. He mopped the sweat from her brow with his handkerchief. Where was that ambulance?

"Pain was awful. Heard the baby cry once. Passed out. Woke up in bed. Baby gone. Saw Mark's face later. Knew Jack must have let it die."

Her breathing became more labored. "Wanted to die. Wanted Jack to die first. Didn't tell Mark."

She licked her lips. "Rested for a couple days. Waited my chance. That night Jack came into my room before he left. Didn't say anything. Just looked at me. Knew what that look meant."

Peggy clinched her fists obviously determined to finish her story.

"Jack came back that night. Forgot pain, how weak I felt…everything but what he'd done. I followed him into the bathroom. Strangled him."

As Peggy described watching Jack's dying face in the mir-

197

ror, Dalton thought Ginger might faint. He squeezed her hand to steady her.

Peggy reached up and gripped Dalton's arm.

"Don't bury me near Jack. Promise."

Before Dalton could answer, her arm dropped to the floor, and she let out a deep sigh. Her eyes were still open, but Dalton knew that Peggy was gone. Ginger leaned against his shoulder.

The rattling of the metal staircase announced the arrival of the paramedics. Mark came in behind the emergency medical crew. As they began to whip out their equipment, Mark tried to kneel down by his sister's body.

"I shouldn't have listened to her. She wanted me to make my deliveries, but I never should have left her. I knew she was getting worse. She wouldn't let me take her to a doctor."

The small kitchen was suddenly overflowing with people and paraphernalia. Dalton and Ginger stood up and moved out of the way. Dalton took Mark by the arm, leading him toward the living room. He motioned for Ginger to follow. The sounds of the paramedic's futile attempts to resuscitate Peggy's breathing filled the apartment.

Dalton escorted the pale and trembling Mark to one end of the couch and sat himself at the other end. Ginger shivered near the fireplace.

The shocked look he saw on his wife's face matched the inward jolt Dalton struggled to ignore while he tried to make sense of the deathbed confession he'd just heard.

All the feelings of respect, friendship, and yes, even the love he'd felt for his old friend had been ripped right out of him, leaving a hole the size of a dump truck inside. How could he not have known, not even suspected what Jack Hatfield had really been like? What kind of investigator was he, not to even have a clue?

The living room seemed lifeless and empty, even with the

three of them sitting there and the paramedics just a few yards away. Dalton didn't want to think about Jack or Peggy, about their sad lives and even sadder deaths; instead he concentrated on trying to figure out how to help the only family member left.

He began to gently explain to Mark that Peggy was dead and that she'd told him what had happened to Jack just before she died. Mark stared at the floor as if in a stupor.

"I'll have to take you to the detention center, Mark, for questioning, but I want you to have a lawyer present when I talk to you officially."

"Are you arresting me?"

"I believe Peggy's statement that you weren't actually involved in killing Jack, but you did move his body. The state's attorney could decide to prosecute you as an accessory after the fact to his murder. You'll need a lawyer to help you sort this out."

Dalton hoped the state's attorney wouldn't decide to prosecute Mark; he'd fight her on that one. Somebody in this nightmare needed a break.

"You think that young fella you told us about would help me?" Mark asked. "He sure was quick to figure out Jack's business stuff for us. I don't know nobody else to ask."

Mark's eyes begged for mercy like a puppy that had done its business in the wrong place and knew it.

"I'm sure he'll be happy to advise you. When we go over in a few minutes, I'll make sure he knows you're there."

Ginger and Dalton exchanged glances. Her eyes mirrored his disillusionment.

"Mark, I'll help you make arrangements for Peggy, if you like," Ginger spoke up. "I think Miss Mamie will help, too."

Mark covered his face with his hands and began to cry. Dalton had no idea what to say to comfort him. Apparently his wife didn't either, so they waited in silence.

Dalton watched the look on Ginger's face evolve into grim determination. Then she squared her shoulders. He was willing to bet she would head straight for her computer when she got home. No big dinner tonight. She'd write a story that would set this town on its collective ear.

CHAPTER 34

A paramedic stepped into the living room and Dalton joined him in the doorway.

"She's gone. Want me to contact the coroner?"

"Jeffords is in Evansville right now, having some tests run for me. Maybe someone else at the funeral home can transport her body there for autopsy. I don't want to just leave her lying on the kitchen floor. Give them a call and see if anyone is available to pick her up."

"Sure."

The coroner would have the pathologist look for any signs of physical or sexual abuse and verify that childbed fever was what really killed Peggy.

If Peggy were the latest victim in this mess, hopefully the pathologist would find all the evidence he needed inside her poor, worn out body. He would be able to confirm Peggy's last statement about Jack's treatment of her and the birth of their baby. The pathologist could add Jack's DNA to the group that was being compared with Baby Doe's and solve that mystery as well. Dalton wanted to be able to completely close all the cases, no loose ends.

A few minutes later the paramedics helped load the body on the stretcher and take it down the steep stairway. Dalton watched the driver turn the funeral home's van around and head down Market Street.

With everyone now gone, Dalton locked the back door and escorted Mark Hatfield to the detention center. They didn't speak most of the way. The afternoon sun over Superman was blinding. Both men shaded their eyes as they trudged toward Dalton's office.

"One question, Mark, and I swear the answer will remain between us, off the record. Why did you hang Jack's body on the statue? Why didn't you just dump it in the river like Peggy told you to? We probably never would have found it there."

Mark turned around to Dalton, a snarl on his face. "Because all my life it's been Jack the football hero; Jack the good family man, taking care of his little brother and sister; Jack the good, honest business man; Jack the super hero. Always Jack, Jack, Jack."

Mark spat on the curb and pulled his hat down tighter on his head.

"I put him up there so everyone in this town could see that he was just a man, not the super hero you all thought he was."

Nearing the statue, Dalton's need to know became overwhelming. "Why didn't you come to me? I could have done something to stop Jack from hurting Peggy."

"You were Jack's best friend. You thought he hung the moon. So did everyone else. I didn't dare trust you. You don't know what he threatened to do if we told."

Mark's voice broke as he continued to describe what Jack had done to Peggy all those years. Seeing it through Mark's eyes chilled Dalton to the bone.

"When Sis was sixteen, Jack made her drop out of school. Guess he was afraid she'd tell someone what he was doing. Lots of times she was too hurt or ashamed to go anyhow."

And no one had questioned her dropping out.

"He hated her, hated all women. Said they were all harlots, only bringing men trouble. Said he was just giving Sis what she deserved. But that ain't true. She never deserved what he did to her." Mark shook his head.

"Jack never let me go near any other women, so I don't know about them. Guess he hated me too. Sis said he was jealous of us, that he didn't want to share our mother with us. I hardly remember my mother." He let out a deep sigh.

How could Dalton have missed seeing all this, either as a teenager or an adult? It had never even occurred to him until now that Jack had been hiding his own deep dark secrets rather than protecting his family when he'd asked his friends to start visiting him downstairs in the hardware store instead of upstairs in the apartment.

Dalton had totally accepted his friend's excuse of wanting to give his sister and brother some needed privacy after their parents' deaths. After a while, the store visits had become habit. How could he have swallowed everything Jack said without question?

"Ruby came by to see me today. She said Jack had started abusing her too, just in the past few months. I didn't want to believe it. Guess I don't have any choice now," Dalton said.

"Jack used Ruby so people would think he was normal. But Sis and I knew how he was. And now everyone in this whole town'll know." Mark stopped to run a fist across his grimy cheek.

"Wish I'd had Sis's guts. Wish I hadn't been so afraid of Jack. I'da killed him a long time ago."

"I just wish I'd known, Mark. Friend or no, I'd never have let Jack hurt Peggy like that."

Mark continued, as if he hadn't heard. "That night, Sis went to bed real early. Said she didn't feel well. Never even crossed my mind that she'd try to kill him."

"What happened?"

"When Jack came home, he went into the bathroom. I heard noises and then a thump. Figured something had happened to her. Sis was standing over Jack's body, laughing.

The look on her face scared me."

He swallowed hard, and Dalton could see the fear was still in his eyes as he remembered.

"Sis helped me wrap Jack in the shower curtain, then I loaded him in the back of the truck like she told me to. I meant to do what she said with his body. I surely did. But when I started for the river, I saw the statue and decided to put him there, so the whole town could see him."

"Why was he wearing his Superman costume?"

"He always liked to wear it on holidays and stuff. Acted so proud. Thought he was so much better than us." Mark shook his head. "Figured his being dead was a real holiday for Sis and me. Served him right to be found that way, wearing that suit. I snuck back into the apartment and got it. Sis was too busy watching out the window for Mamie Timsley to notice me."

"Peggy put on your hat and clothes and sat on the couch like you always do. You both knew Miss Mamie kept an eye on your apartment, right?" Dalton asked.

"Yeah. Sis figured she'd give us an alibi. I came back in through the kitchen. Sis never knew. Then I got the saw out from under the sink. I lied when I said we didn't keep no tools upstairs. Didn't want you looking under there."

Dalton couldn't believe what he was hearing.

"What on earth made you cut off Jack's head?"

"Everyone thinks I'm dumb, but I figured that one out all by myself. I thought you wouldn't be able to tell he was strangled if I cut through that line on his neck. When I got back downstairs, I dressed Jack in that stupid suit, then I wrapped him up again. I keep a rain suit behind the truck seat. Put it on to keep the blood off my clothes."

Mark was nearly on target. The decapitation had removed all but one small part of the strangulation mark on Jack's neck. He couldn't have known that other body signs would point to the actual cause of death. And his use of the shower curtain and rain suit had effectively kept Dalton's office from discovering exactly where the murder had taken place until now.

"I drove back to the statue. Then I cut off Jack's head and put it where he could look at Superman. I used the janitor's ladder to get his body on the statue's arm where everybody could see it."

"What did you do with the saw?"

"I wrapped everything in the shower curtain, put a rock in it like Sis told me to, and took it down to the river. You'll never find it. Current's too fast. I wore gloves, like they do on TV. But I had to throw away my new tennis shoes. Got blood all over 'em."

He paused and looked up at the statue. Dalton followed his gaze.

"I was so happy at first, knowing Jack would never be able to hurt Sis again. He killed the baby, too." Mark paused and looked straight into Dalton's eyes.

"When I got back home the night it was born, I could tell by the look on Jack's face. He made me bury the poor little thing, said he'd do worse to Sis if I didn't."

Dalton realized Jack had sent his brother to Paducah the night the baby was born to get him out of the way. He hadn't wanted any interference with his plans.

"Jack must've done something to Sis when the baby came. She was never right after that. Started getting real sick. Must've done something to the baby, too. There was an awful lot of blood."

"The baby bled to death through the umbilical cord because Jack didn't tie it off. Part of the other end of the cord, the afterbirth, stayed inside Peggy."

No use sugar coating it, the truth was bound to come out eventually. "It became infected, and that's what killed her. A doctor would have made sure that the cord was tied off and that all the afterbirth came out. Neither of them would have died if Jack had just taken Peggy to a doctor."

"Things seemed so good with Jack gone, but it didn't last long. Big Ed was hiding in the bushes and saw me that night. It was really cold. Never figured he'd be out on the street on a night like that." Mark shivered slightly.

"Big Ed said he'd keep quiet if I gave him money. I didn't have none, so I went to Sis." He shook his head sadly.

"She said she'd meet Big Ed in my place. She didn't want me to mess things up like I had with Jack's body. She was pretty ticked about that. Never dreamed she'd kill Big Ed, though."

Dalton could easily imagine it. Peggy's back had been to the wall, and having killed once, she wouldn't have found it that much harder the second time.

"Big Ed was surprised when she showed up instead of me, but she told him she was the only one who could get cash out of the store. Sis told me later that she held out some money, and then let it drop on the steps. He was so greedy he reached right down and scooped it up. Guess he never thought a woman would hit 'im."

Dalton wouldn't have thought it either. But Peggy had been big, and fairly strong, in spite of her illness.

"She hit that old drunk as hard as she could with the hammer Jack kept in the toolbox under the sink. He fell on top of the money. She had to get it back. That twenty bucks was all we had right then."

Twenty bucks. Big Ed had died for a measly twenty dollars.

"She dropped the hammer and rolled him over to get the money out from under him. When she stood up, she got dizzy. Sis was pretty sick by then. She thought she heard a noise in the apartment upstairs, so she lit out for home, forgetting the hammer."

Dalton had wondered why the murder weapon had been left behind.

"By the time Sis got home, she was too sick to talk. When she remembered the hammer, you guys were all over the place, and it was too late for either of us to go back. Sis told me all about it the next morning. She was wearing gloves, so she didn't think you'd be able to prove it was our hammer."

Dalton turned away from the statue and looked at the Lipinski's stairwell. If Big Ed hadn't gotten greedy, he'd still be alive. If he'd told the sheriff's office what he'd known right away, Peggy's condition would have come out much sooner, possibly in time for medical treatment to save her. What a waste. Dalton turned his attention back to Mark.

"I didn't know what to do. I just prayed we wouldn't get caught. Guess my prayer wasn't answered." Mark scuffed his foot on the curb.

"Least ways Sis won't have to go to jail."

Mark shoved his hands in his pockets and started across the street. Dalton had nothing to say in the face of all that anger and grief. He thought about what Wilson had said, that it was hard for men to really understand how terrible sexual abuse was for a woman.

Standing in the shadow of the huge statue where the mystery first began, Dalton's head swam at the thought of all the questions answered and all the ones that would never be answered.

He had the solutions to all three murders, four if you counted Peggy because Jack Hatfield had surely murdered his sister as well as his own child by refusing them medical care. The answers didn't please him any more than the questions had. And they certainly wouldn't please the locals who'd been demanding those same answers from him.

What could he have done differently? For the life of him, he couldn't think of a single thing. And yet, his best friend, his best friend's sister, an innocent child, and an old drunk were all dead.

Mark was right about one thing, no one in this town would ever think of Jack Hatfield as a superhero again.

Dalton glanced up at the giant statue and did a double take. He could have sworn Superman had just nodded at him. Nah, must've been a trick of the light. The sun was right in his eyes. Dalton turned on his heel and followed Mark into the detention center.

THE END

COMING SOON

MURDER BEYOND METROPOLIS

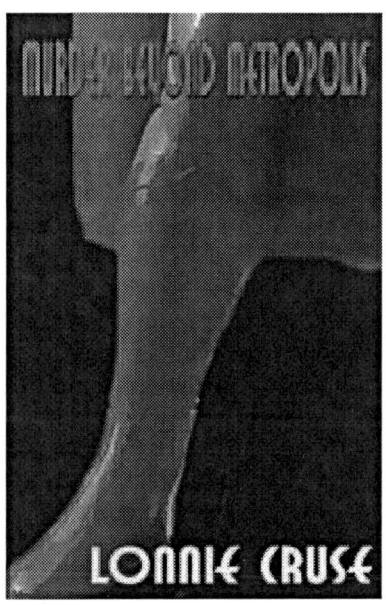

ENJOY A SNEEK PREVIEW OF THE NEXT BOOK IN THE SERIES
MURDER BEYOND METROPOLIS $24.95
ISBN 0-9749608-7-X
AVAIALBLE IN HARDCOVER
SUMMER 2004

Chapter 1

Sheriff Joe Dalton shoved his fists deeper into the pockets of his jeans in a serious effort to keep from strangling either the rooster or his wife, Ginger. Trudging toward the back of the yard, he shot an angry glance at her pretty, freckle-spattered face.

"I suppose you think this is funny?"

He heard another snicker escape between the teeth clamped firmly onto her lower lip.

Dalton glared down at the rooster frantically flogging his calf and pecking at the back of his knees in an apparent effort to run the big stranger out of his territory. Obviously Ginger didn't pose as much of a threat to the fowl as he did.

Dalton longed to give the little Banty a good swift kick, but didn't dare with Ginger watching. Shame she wasn't quite as tenderhearted about husbands as she was children and animals.

"I was perfectly happy with the view of Mary Sue's new hen house from the kitchen window, but, no, she has to shove me outside to get a closer look," Dalton said.

"Maybe you should arrest her for assault with a deadly chicken?" Ginger's previously discreet snicker now erupted into a full-scale giggle.

Dalton rolled his eyes. "Let's just get this over with and go back inside for breakfast. I can smell the country ham frying clear out here."

The new hen house, a combination of old barn wood and chicken wire, had the country look his niece seemed so fond of. The low-slung structure bordered a narrow gravel alley that separated it from the houses behind.

To the left of the hen house, the yard sported a freshly tilled garden that would soon be full of vegetables. To the right, Mary Sue's flower garden, already abloom with the tall spikes of spring, helped to disguise part of the unattractive chicken wire pen attached to the hen house. Dalton couldn't have identified those flowers if his life depended on it, but his wife could, and he prayed Mary Sue wouldn't offer to separate them and share starters with Ginger. The joy of digging holes and planting flowers was only surpassed by a trip to the dentist in Dalton's opinion.

Just a few more feet and he would be able to step between the flowerbed and the pen, take a quick peek inside the hen house, and be on his way.

Dalton rounded the corner of the flower bed, still looking behind him at the rooster, caught the toe of his boot on the edge of a bundle lying there, and fell with a splat into a large pile of chicken droppings.

He leaped up off the ground and rounded on his wife, intending to give her a double-barrel shot of temper if she dared to laugh at him.

The horrified look on her face stopped him cold. Dalton figured he must have somehow managed to hit the offending fowl with his huge boot and lost his balance, coming down like a dead tree in a windstorm.

He wiped his hands on his pants, glanced toward the ground, and groped for some excuse to explain his clumsiness in squashing the little fowl. Wait a second. That bundle was way too big to be a rooster. It looked more like a large laundry bundle. What was it doing there? The clothesline was clear on the other side of the yard, near the back door.

He reached down to pick up the bundle and a tuft of white hair caught his eye. This was a body, not a laundry bundle. Anybody that still had to be dead.

Without hope of finding a pulse, he touched the grayish neck. Rigor mortis held the body firmly in its death position.

Dalton turned back to his wife. She looked as sick as he felt. His cell phone sat unused in his shirt pocket. Best get Ginger back into the house and let her make the call. It would keep her busy, and the rest of their family inside. No use having half a dozen relatives trooping all over the backyard, destroying any possible evidence left behind.

"Go inside and tell Mary Sue to call nine-one-one. Have the dispatcher alert the Brookport police chief, the coroner, and the crime lab." Ginger started toward the house without a word. Dalton called after her.

"Tell the dispatcher to send out any available deputies. And make sure everyone stays inside with you."

He watched Ginger move toward the old, blue clapboard house, and waited for the metallic squeal of protest as she opened the screen door. Only then did he kneel down and turn his attention back to the body. His first glance had been brief, but his instincts had told him that his niece's quiet backyard had just become a crime scene.

The long, narrow backyard was fairly standard for a small town. A huge oak to one side provided some shade from the early morning sun, for which he was thankful. He was probably going to be out there for a while.

The tiny old woman lay on her side, tightly scrunched into the fetal position, her arms and hands covered with small blood spots, probably the result of defending herself from a pecking attack. The possible culprit hovered nearby.

Dalton noted that the woman's eyes were squeezed tightly shut as if in fear, and her elbows and knees were covered with dried blood. The huge gash on top of her head could have happened in a fall, but he'd bet dollars to donuts someone had hit her, and she'd crawled here, collapsed, and died. But from where had she come?

His glance followed a trail of blood leading away from her back toward the alley, and out of sight.

The screen door squealed. Dalton turned toward the sound and met with the unwelcome sight of his niece's five-year-old son, Leonard, sneaking out the back door. Leonard was a bright, active little boy, with the same coppery hair and splatter of freckles as Dalton's wife. Family sentiments about the boy's future were firmly divided into two camps, half thinking he was destined for the president's chair in the Oval Office, the other half equally certain that he was headed straight for the electric chair. Dalton's sympathies lay heavily in the direction of the electric chair faction.

"Go back inside, Leonard, and stay with your Momma. You can't come out here right now."

"Momma said I could. She said you might need some help."

Dalton suspected Mary Sue had said no such thing.

"Not right now. Go back inside and tell your Momma to make

more coffee. We're about to get a lot of company."

"But Umple Joe, Momma said I could." As he spoke, Leonard moved down the few steps from the door and stood on the cracked sidewalk leading toward Dalton.

Time for action. With the arrival of the newcomer, the rooster had turned its attention away from pecking Dalton's leg to Leonard standing on the sidewalk. Dalton swooped over, grabbed the Banty, and held it toward Leonard.

"You know what? Your Momma's right. I could use some help. This rooster is pecking the daylights out of me. You come hold him while I open the pen door, and we'll put him inside. He probably won't hurt you."

Leonard shot up the stairs and through the screen door, whining "Momma," all the way. Dalton eyed the captive rooster. The rooster eyed him back. He carried the over-eager yard guard a couple of steps to the wire chicken pen, opened the door, and set him gently inside. A cloud of feathers and an instantaneous cacophony of squawks came from the regular inhabitants.

"Sorry," Dalton said to the rooster, "but you'll be much safer in there with them."

Dalton dusted off his hands again and stooped near the body. The sound of crunching gravel in the driveway turned him back around. That had better not be Leonard trying a different route.

He was relieved to see rookie officer Doug Hollenback from the Brookport Police Department round the side of the old house and head toward him. The radio at Hollenback's hip crackled, and he reached to turn it down.

Dalton couldn't help noticing the young officer's dark uniform didn't have a wrinkle or a spot of sweat on it despite the warm, muggy morning. His own off-duty jeans and pullover looked like they'd just come out of the washer, wet and wrinkled. Dust and chicken droppings scattered here and there did little to improve his appearance. His uniform often looked the same, whatever the weather.

"'Lo, Sheriff. Heard on the radio there's a problem here. The chief is out of town on vacation. Thought I'd better run over and see what's up." His dark eyes flashed over the yard.

The young officer reached the flowerbed and stopped short at the sight of the old woman behind it. He swallowed hard.

"That's Miss Lacy Spanner. What happened to her?" Hollenback ran a hand through buzzed black hair that matched the uniform.

"The coroner will have to tell us for sure. You know her personally?"

"Sure. Everybody in Brookport knows her. She taught third grade at the elementary school a block over." Hollenback tipped his head in that direction.

"She retired several years ago. Anyone who went to school before Miss Spanner retired had her as a teacher. She was one tough cookie, but she sure was good. Nobody messed with her much." The young officer shook his head. "I can't believe she's dead."

"She doesn't look very tough right now. She's been dead for several hours. It looks to me like someone hit her over the head." Dalton pointed to the head injury.

"I don't see her getting a cut like that from a fall. It looks like she tried to crawl for help. Didn't she have a telephone?" Dalton asked.

"Nope. She hated phones. Said she only got calls from telemarketers."

The young cop reached for his notebook. "Neighbors usually check on her every day. We stop by on patrol now and then, but I haven't seen her for a few days."

He flipped a couple of pages in the notebook. "No record of any recent problems at her place that I see. She lives just across the alley, one door down. Wonder why she crawled here instead of to the next door neighbors'?"

Dalton wondered the same thing. "Maybe you can check with the neighbors for us and see if they heard anything. Meantime, if you have some tape in your patrol car, I'll rope this area off."

"Sure. I'll help you, then I'll walk down the alley and see what I can find out."

Hollenback retrieved the tape from his patrol car. Dalton reached for the roll of bright yellow tape and noticed a partially bandaged burn on the young rookie's left wrist and hand.

"You tangle with a hot stove?" he asked.

"Worse, a hot coffee pot. The glass carafe shattered, dumping the contents on my arm. I'd barely tapped it against the cup, but I guess that was just one bump too many."

"Looks painful," Dalton said.

"The ER doc gave me some salve. As long as I keep the air out with the medicine and the bandage, it isn't too bad."

Dalton tied one end of the tape to the door of the hen house, setting off the inhabitants again, wound it around the tree at the edge of the property where the tire swing hung, and walked it to the edge of the alley where he met Hollenback tying his end of the tape to the post that held Mary Sue's trash cans securely. They had created a good size square for the crime lab team to work with.

Dalton turned to the rookie. "I'll cordon off this end of the alley. You take the rest of the tape with you and cordon off the other end. We don't need the neighbors wandering through here until the crime lab team has finished their investigation."

"Sure thing."

Hollenback crunched down the alley following the trail of blood. Dalton noted a window full of eyes watching the activity from Mary Sue's kitchen.

Dalton finished cordoning off his end of the alley, stepped back into the yard, and barely avoided colliding with the short stocky body of Massac County Coroner Don Jeffords.

"Any idea who the victim is?" The coroner squatted for a closer look at the body. Dalton watched over Jeffords' shoulder as he worked.

"Lacy Spanner," Dalton answered. "Retired school teacher, lives just over yonder."

Dalton looked down at the body. How small and fragile she seemed. Hard to imagine that she had once struck fear in her students. Elderly people should be able to die in bed with some dignity, not shriveled up at the edge of a chicken pen.

Another crunch of gravel in the driveway announced the arrival of two of Dalton's deputies. He left the coroner to his examination.

Deputy Linda Peters strode across the grassy area, her blonde ponytail swinging under her brown uniform hat, and generous-sized shirt heaving. Craig Edwards' skeletal figure loped along just behind her.

"Heard you found a body, Boss. Wilson and Jenson are investigating a one-vehicle accident on Mount Mission Road. A farmer ran off the shoulder and dumped a load of hay everywhere. They're trying to get it cleaned up," Peters offered.

Dalton grunted. He was about to bark out orders to the deputies when the young Brookport rookie came jogging back.

"Rear door of the victim's house is wide open," Hollenback huffed. "It looks like a tornado hit the kitchen area. I didn't go in any farther, thought I'd better come tell you. Could be a burglary gone wrong."

"Thanks. I'll go back with you and have a look," Dalton replied.

The small city of Brookport had its own police department, but Dalton's office in nearby Metropolis covered most of the crime in Massac County. With the chief away, he'd decided to take on this investigation personally, and see it through to the end.

He turned back to his deputies. "You two keep everyone out of the crime scene area until the techs arrive. If Leonard sticks his head out the back door again, feel free to shoot first and ask questions later."

Deputy Linda Peters grinned. Dalton followed Hollenback down the alley, trying to ignore the burning sensation in his gut that usually meant no matter how bad things were they were probably going to get worse. Much worse.

Printed in the United States
39966LVS00004B/259-288

9 780974 960890